Thierry p… leaned cl… couldn't s… ere's something I want you to do.”

“There is?” Imogen couldn't imagine what. Unless of course, it was the DNA test to prove paternity. She'd heard there were risks involved with those during pregnancy, but if it meant giving her child a secure future—

“Yes.” He paused so long, tension tightened the bare skin of her shoulders. “I want you to marry me.”

“What did you say?” Her voice was a croak from constricted muscles.

“I want us to marry. This week.”

He looked so relaxed, as if he'd merely commented on the quality of the meal they'd shared, or on the beautiful old buildings floodlit along the banks of the Seine.

Her pulse fluttered like a mad thing. “You can't be serious.”

“Never more so.”

That was when she saw it, the glint of determination in those espresso-dark eyes.

One Night With Consequences

When one night...leads to pregnancy!

When succumbing to a night of unbridled desire, it's impossible to think past the morning after!

But with the sheets barely settled, that little blue line appears on the pregnancy test, and it doesn't take long to realize that one night of white-hot passion has turned into a lifetime of consequences!

Only one question remains:

How do you tell a man you've just met that you're about to share more than just his bed?

Find out in:

Prince Nadir's Secret Heir by Michelle Conder

Carrying the Greek's Heir by Sharon Kendrick

Married for Amari's Heir by Maisey Yates

Bound by the Billionaire's Baby by Cathy Williams

From One Night to Wife by Rachael Thomas

Her Nine Month Confession by Kim Lawrence

An Heir Fit for a King by Abby Green

Larenzo's Christmas Baby by Kate Hewitt

An Illicit Night with the Greek by Susanna Carr

Look for more ***One Night With Consequences*** coming soon!

If you missed any of these fabulous stories, they can be found at Harlequin.com

Annie West

A VOW TO SECURE HIS LEGACY

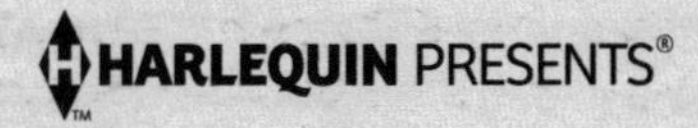

ISBN-13: 978-0-373-13419-9

A Vow to Secure His Legacy

First North American Publication 2016

This edition published by arrangement with Harlequin Books S.A.

For questions and comments about the quality of this book, please contact us at CustomerService@Harlequin.com.

Printed in U.S.A.

Growing up near the beach, **Annie West** spent lots of time observing tall, burnished lifeguards—early research! Now she spends her days fantasizing about gorgeous men and their love lives. Annie has been a reader all her life. She also loves travel, long walks, good company and great food. You can contact her at annie@annie-west.com, or via PO Box 1041, Warners Bay, NSW 2282, Australia.

Books by Annie West

Harlequin Presents

Seducing His Enemy's Daughter
Damasco Claims His Heir
Imprisoned by a Vow
Captive in the Spotlight
Defying Her Desert Duty
Prince of Scandal

Seven Sexy Sins

The Sinner's Marriage Redemption

Desert Vows

The Sheikh's Princess Bride
The Sultan's Harem Bride

At His Service

An Enticing Debt to Pay

Dark-Hearted Tycoons

Undone by His Touch

Sinful Desert Nights

Girl in the Bedouin Tent

Visit the Author Profile page at Harlequin.com for more titles.

Dedicated to those who work with
the sick and frail:

medical staff, technicians, administrative staff,
care workers, paramedics and volunteers.

Your skills and above all your kindness
make such a difference!

Thanks, too, to the lovely Fabiola Chenet
for your advice. Any errors are all mine!

PROLOGUE

'IMOGEN! WHAT A lovely surprise.' The receptionist looked up from her desk. 'I didn't expect to see you again.' She paused, her smile fading. 'I was so sorry to hear about your mother.'

Her voice held a note of sympathy that stirred grief, even after four months. It was like pressure applied to a bruise that hadn't faded. The pain was more intense today because coming here, doing this, was so difficult. Imogen laced her fingers together to stop them trembling.

'Thanks, Krissy.' The staff here at the specialist's consulting rooms had been terrific with her mum and her.

Imogen swept her gaze around the familiar space. The soothing sea-green furnishings, the vase of bright gerberas on the counter and the waiting room of people apparently engrossed in their magazines. She recognised their alert stillness—a desperate attempt to pretend everything would be all right. That they'd receive good news from the doctor, despite the fact he had a reputation for dealing with the most difficult cases.

Her stomach swooped in a nauseating loop-the-loop. A chill skated up her spine to clamp her neck.

Swiftly, she turned back to the desk.

'What brings you here?' Krissy leaned in. 'You just can't stay away, is that it? You love our company so much?'

Imogen opened her mouth but her throat constricted. No words came out.

'Krissy! That's enough.' It was Ruby, the older receptionist, bustling in from a back room. She wore an expression of careful serenity. Only the sympathetic look in those piercing eyes gave anything away. 'Ms Holgate is here for an appointment.'

There was a hiss of indrawn breath and a clatter as Krissy dropped the stapler she'd been holding.

'Please take a seat, Ms Holgate. The doctor is running a little late. There was a delay in surgery this morning, but he'll see you shortly.'

'Thanks,' Imogen croaked and turned away with a vague smile in Krissy's direction. She couldn't meet the other woman's eyes. They'd be round with shock. Perhaps even with the horror she'd seen in her own mirror.

For weeks she'd told herself she was imagining things... that the symptoms would pass. Until her GP had looked at her gravely, barely concealing concern, and said he was sending her for tests. Then he'd referred her to the very man who'd tried to save her mother when she'd suffered exactly the same symptoms.

Imogen had had the tests last week and all this week she'd waited for a message from her GP saying there was no need to see the specialist, that everything was clear.

There'd been no message. No reprieve. No good news.

She swallowed hard and made herself cross the room, taking a seat where she could look out at the bright Sydney sunshine rather than at the reception desk.

Pride dictated she play the game, hiding her fear behind a façade of calm. She took a magazine, not looking at the cover. She wouldn't take it in. Her brain was too busy cataloguing all the reasons this couldn't end well.

A year ago she'd have believed everything would be okay.

But too much had happened in her twenty-fifth year for her to be complacent ever again. The world had shifted on its axis, proving once more, as it had in childhood, that nothing was safe, nothing sure.

Nine months ago had come the news that her twin sister—flamboyant, full-of-life Isabelle—was dead. She'd survived paragliding, white-water rafting and backpacking through Africa, only to be knocked over by a driver in Paris as she crossed the street on her way to work.

Imogen swallowed down a knot of grief. Isabelle had accused her of being in a rut, of playing safe when there was a wide world out there to be explored and enjoyed.

Her twin had followed her dream, even knowing the odds of her succeeding were a million to one. Yet she *had* succeeded. She'd moved to France and through talent, perseverance plus sheer luck had snaffled a job with a top fashion designer. She'd had everything to look forward to. Then suddenly her life was snuffed out.

Soon after had come their mother's diagnosis—a brain tumour. Massive, risky to operate on, lethal.

Blindly, Imogen flipped open the magazine on her lap.

When the news had come from Paris she'd protested that there must have been a mistake—Isabelle couldn't possibly be dead. It had taken weeks to accept the truth. Then, as her mother's headaches and blurry vision had worsened and the doctors looked more and more grim, Imogen had been convinced there would be a cure. Fatal brain tumours just didn't happen in her world. The diagnosis was impossible.

Until the impossible had happened and she was left alone, bereft of the only two people in the world who'd loved her.

The past nine months had shown her how possible the impossible actually was.

And now there was her own illness. No mistaking this for anything other than the disease that had struck down her mother. She'd been with her mum as her illness had progressed. She knew every stage, every symptom.

How much longer did she have? Seven months? Nine? Or would the tumour be more aggressive in a younger woman?

Imogen turned a page and lifted her eyes, scanning the room. Was this her destiny? To become a regular here until they admitted there was nothing they could do for her? To become another statistic in the health-care system?

Isabelle's voice sounded in her head.

You need to get out and live, Imogen. Try something new, take a risk, enjoy yourself. Life is for living!

Imogen snorted. What chance would she have for living now?

She thought of the dreams she'd nurtured, planning and carefully executing every step. Working her way through university. Getting a job. Building professional success. Saving for a flat. Finding a nice, reliable, loving man who'd stick by her as their father hadn't. A man who'd want a lifetime with her. They'd see all the things Isabelle had raved about. The northern lights in Iceland. Venice's Grand Canal. And Paris. Paris with the man she loved.

Imogen blinked and looked down. Open on her lap was a double-page photo of Paris at sunset. Her breath hitched, a frisson of obscure excitement stirring her blood.

The panorama was as spectacular as Isabelle had said.

Imogen's throat burned as she remembered how she'd turned down her sister's invitation, saying she'd visit when she had a deposit saved for a flat and had helped their mum finish that long-overdue kitchen renovation.

Isabelle had ribbed her about planning her life to the nth degree. But Imogen had always needed security. She couldn't drop everything and gallivant off to Paris.

Fat lot of good that will do you now you're dying. What will you do, spend your money on a great coffin?

Imogen gazed at the Seine, copper-bright in the afternoon light. Her stare shifted to the Eiffel Tower, a glittering invitation. *You'd love it, Ginny—gorgeous and gaudy by night but just so...Paris!*

She'd spent her life playing safe. Avoiding risk, working hard, denying herself the adventures Isabelle revelled in, because she planned to do that later.

There'd be no later. There was only now.

Imogen wasn't aware of getting up, but she found herself striding across the room and out into the sunlight. A voice called but she didn't look back.

She didn't have much time. She refused to spend it in hospitals and waiting rooms until she absolutely had to.

For once she'd forget being sensible. Forget caution. She intended to *live*.

CHAPTER ONE

'TELL ME, *MA CHÉRIE,* will you be at the resort when we visit? It would be so much more convenient having the owner on the premises when we do the promotional photo shoot.' Her voice was intimately pitched, reaching him easily despite the chatter of the crowd in the hotel's grand reception room.

Thierry looked down into the publicist's face, reading the invitation in her eyes.

She was beautiful, sophisticated and, he guessed by the way she licked her bottom lip and pressed her slim frame closer, ready to be very accommodating. Yet he felt no flicker of excitement.

Excitement! He'd left that behind four years ago. Would he even recognise it after all this time?

Bitterness filled his mouth. He'd been living a half-life, hemmed in by conference-room walls and duty, forcing himself to care about minutiae that held no intrinsic interest. *Except those details had meant the difference between salvaging the family's foundering business portfolio and losing it.*

'I haven't decided. There are things I need to sort out here in Paris.'

But soon… A few months and he'd hand over the business to his cousin Henri and, more importantly, the managers Thierry had hand-picked. They'd guide Henri and maintain all Thierry had achieved, securing the Girard family fortune and leaving him free at last.

'Think about it, Thierry.' Her lips formed a glossy pout as she swayed close. 'It would be very…agreeable.'

'Of course I will. The idea is very tempting.'

But not enough, he realised with abrupt clarity, to drag

him from Paris. These meetings would bring him closer to divesting himself of his burdens. That held far more allure than the prospect of sex with a svelte blonde.

Hell! He was turning into a cold-blooded corporate type. Since when had his libido taken second place to business?

Except his libido wasn't involved. That was the shocking thing. At thirty-four Thierry was in his prime. He enjoyed sex and his success with women showed he had a talent, even a reputation, for it. Yet he felt nothing when this gorgeous woman invited him into her bed.

Hadn't he known taking on the family business would destroy him? It was sucking the life out of him. It was…

His gaze locked on a figure on the far side of the room, and his thoughts blurred. His pulse accelerated and his chest expanded as he hefted a startled breath.

His companion murmured something and stretched up to kiss his cheek. Automatically, Thierry returned the salutation, responding to her farewell as she joined a group who'd just entered the hotel ballroom.

Instantly, his gaze swung back to the far side of the room. The woman who'd caught his eye stood poised, her weight on one foot, as if about to leave.

He was already pushing his way through the crowd when she straightened and drew back her shoulders. Delectable, creamy shoulders they were, completely bared by that strapless dress. The white material was lustrous in the light of the chandeliers, drawing a man's eyes to the way it fitted her breasts and small waist like a glove before flaring in an ultra-feminine swirl to the floor.

Thierry swallowed, his throat dry despite the champagne he'd drunk. A familiar tightness in his groin assured him that his libido was alive and kicking after all. Yet he barely registered relief. He was too busy drinking her in.

In a room packed with little black dresses and sleek, glittery outfits, this woman stood out like *grand cru* from cheap table wine.

She turned her head, presenting him with an engaging profile, and Thierry realised she was speaking. He halted, surprised that his walk had lengthened to an urgent stride.

Her companion was a gamine-faced woman, pointing out people to the woman in white. The woman in white and scarlet, he amended, taking in the pattern of red flowers cascading around her as she moved. There was white and scarlet on her arms too. She wore long gloves to her elbows, reminding him of photos he'd seen of his *grand-mère* at balls and parties decades ago.

Thierry's gut clenched as the woman lifted one gloved hand to her throat in a curiously nervous gesture. Who knew gloves could be erotic? But there was no mistaking the weighted feeling in his lower body. He imagined stripping the glove down her arm, centimetre by slow centimetre, kissing his way to her fingers before divesting her of that dress and starting on her body.

Why was she nervous? A shy woman wouldn't wear such a glorious, blatantly sexy concoction.

Heat sparked. His gaze roved her dark, glossy hair swept up from a slim neck. She had full red lips, a retroussé nose and heart-shaped face. Curves that made him ache to touch.

She wasn't just pretty; she was sexy on a level he couldn't resist.

The old Thierry Girard wasn't dead after all.

'You're sure you don't mind?' Saskia sounded doubtful.

Imogen smiled. 'Of course not. I appreciate all you've done these past few days but I'm fine. I'll drink champagne and meet interesting people and enjoy myself.' If she said it enough she might stop being daunted by the glittering crowd long enough to believe it. 'Now go.' She made a shooing gesture, nodding towards the knot of fashion buyers Saskia had pointed out. 'Make the most of this opportunity.'

'Well, for half an hour. I'll look for you then.'

Imogen blinked, overwhelmed anew by the kindness of her sister Isabelle's best friend. Saskia had not only shown her where Izzy had worked and lived, but shared stories about their time together, filling the black well of Imogen's grief with tales that had made Imogen smile for the first time in months.

Saskia had even presented her with the dresses Izzy had made for herself, eye-catching outfits Imogen would never have considered wearing. But here, in Paris, it felt right, a homage to her talented sister. Imogen smoothed her hand down the fabulous satin dress.

'Don't be silly. Go and mingle, Saskia. I don't expect to see you again tonight.' She smiled, making a fair attempt at Izzy's bantering tone, even tilting her head to mimic her sister. 'Since you snaffled me an invitation, I intend to make the most of my only society event. I don't need you cramping my style.'

'Isabelle said you weren't good with lots of new people but obviously you've changed.' Saskia's lips twitched. 'Okay. But join me if you want. I'll be around.'

Imogen kept her smile in place as Saskia left, ignoring the trepidation that rose at being alone, adrift in this sea of beautiful people.

Stupid. This isn't alone. Alone is discovering you're dying and there's no one left in the world who loves you enough to feel more than pity.

Imogen shoved aside the thought. She refused to retreat into self-pity. She was in Paris. She'd make the most of every moment of the next six weeks—Paris, Venice, London, even Reykjavik. She'd wring every drop of joy from each experience before she returned home to face the inevitable.

She swung around, her full-length skirt swishing around her legs, and refused to feel out of place because other women were in cocktail dresses. Isabelle's dress was too wonderful not to wear.

'Puis-je vous offrir du champagne?' The deep, alluring voice sent heat straight to the pit of her stomach, as if she'd inadvertently taken a gulp of whisky.

French was a delicious language. But surely it had been designed for a voice like this? A voice that sent shivers of sensual pleasure across her skin.

She jerked her head around and then up.

Something she couldn't identify slammed into her. Shock? Awareness? Recognition?

How had she not seen him before? He stood out from the crowd. Not just because of his height but because of his sheer presence. Her skin prickled as if she'd walked into a force field.

She met eyes the colour of rich coffee, dark and inviting, and her pulse pounded high in her throat as if her heart had dislodged and tried to escape. Deep-set eyes crinkled at the corners, fanning tiny lines in a tanned face. A man more at home outdoors than at a fashionable party?

Except his tall frame was relaxed, as if he wore a perfect dinner jacket every night to mingle with a who's who of French society. His mouth curled up in a tantalising almost-smile that invited her to smile back. Was that why her lips tingled?

Dark hair, long enough to hint at tousled thickness. A determined chin. Strong cheekbones that made her think of princes, balls and half-forgotten nonsense.

Imogen swallowed, the muscles in her throat responding jerkily. She cleared her throat.

'Je suis désolée, je ne parle pas français.' It was one of her few textbook phrases.

'You don't speak French? Shall we try English?' His voice was just as attractive when he spoke English with that sensuous blurring accent. Pleasure tickled Imogen's backbone, and her stomach clenched.

'How did you guess? Am I that obvious?'

'Not at all.' His gaze did a quick, comprehensive sweep

from her head to her hem that ignited a slow burn deep inside. A burn that transferred to her cheeks as his eyes met hers and something passed between them, as tangible as the beat of her heart. 'You are utterly delightful and feminine but not obvious.'

Imogen felt the corners of her mouth lift. Flirting with a Frenchman. There was one to cross off her bucket list. Back home she hadn't been good at flirtation, but here it seemed she didn't have to do anything at all.

'Who are you?' Funny the way dying helped you overcome a lifetime's reserve. Once she'd have been too overawed to speak to a man who looked so stunningly male. He was one of the most attractive men she'd ever met and despite that aura of latent power he was definitely the most suave. Even that prominent nose looked perfect in his proud face. Just as well his eyes danced or he'd be too daunting.

'My apologies.' He inclined his head in a half-bow that was wholly European and totally charming. 'My name is Thierry Girard.'

'Thierry.' She tried it on her tongue. It didn't sound the same as when he said it. She couldn't quite get the little breath of air after the T, but she liked it.

'And you are?' He stepped closer, his gaze intent. She caught a scent that made her think of mountains—of clear air and pine trees.

'I'm Imogen Holgate.'

'Imogen.' He nodded. 'A pretty name. It suits you.'

Pretty? She hadn't been called that in ages. The last person to do so had been her mum, trying to persuade her into bright colours, saying she hid behind the dark suits she wore for work.

'And now, Imogen, would you like some champagne?' He lifted a glass.

'I can get my own.' She turned to look for a waiter.

'But I brought it especially for you.' She looked down and realised he was holding two glasses, not one. This stranger had singled her out in a room of elegant women and brought her champagne? For a moment she just stared. It was so different from her world, where she paid her way and never had to field compliments from men about anything other than her work.

He raised the other glass, giving her a choice of either. His eyes turned serious. 'Whichever you prefer.'

Her cheeks flushed. He thought she was stalling because she didn't trust him. In case he'd slipped something into one of the glasses.

It was the sort of thing that would have occurred to her once, for in her real life she was always cautious. But right now she was struggling to absorb the fact she was with the most charming, attractive man she'd ever met. The fact that he offered both reassured her.

She took a glass, meeting his eyes, ignoring the tingly sensation where their fingers brushed. 'Is it champagne from the Champagne region?'

'Of course. That's the only wine that can use the name. You like champagne?'

'I've never tried it.'

He blinked, astonishment on his face. *'Vraiment?'*

'Really.' Imogen smiled at his shock. 'I'm from Australia.'

'No, no.' He shook his head. 'I happen to know the Australians import French wine as well as exporting theirs. Champagne travels the world.'

She shrugged, enjoying his disbelief. 'That doesn't mean I've drunk it.' She eyed the wine with excitement. What better place to taste her first champagne than Paris?

'In that case, the occasion deserves a toast. To new friends.' His smile transformed his face from fascinating to magnetic. Imogen inhaled sharply, her lungs pushing at her ribcage. Her fingers tightened on the glass. That smile, this man, made her feel acutely aware of herself as a woman with desires she'd all but forgotten.

Stop it! You've seen men smile before.

Not like this. This was like standing in a shaft of sunshine. And it was an amazing antidote to the chill weight of despair. How could she dwell on despair when he looked at her that way?

She lifted her glass. 'And to new experiences.'

She sipped, feeling the effervescence on the roof of her mouth. 'I like that it's not too sweet. I can taste…pears, is it?'

He drank too, and she was riveted by the sight of his strong throat and the ripple of movement as he swallowed.

Imogen frowned. There was nothing sexy about a man's throat. Was there? There never had been before and she worked surrounded by men.

But none of them were Thierry Girard.

'You're right. Definitely pears.' He watched her over the rim of the glass. 'To new experiences? You have some planned?'

Imogen shrugged. 'A few.'

'Tell me.' When she hesitated he added, 'Please. I'd like to know.'

'Why?' The word shot out, and she caught her bottom lip between her teeth. Typical of her to sound gauche rather than sophisticated. She just wasn't used to male attention. She was the serious, reserved sister, not the gregarious one with a flock of admirers.

'Because I'm interested in you.'

'Seriously?' As soon as the word escaped heat scalded her throat and face. She squeezed her eyes shut. 'Tell me I didn't say that.'

A rich chuckle snagged at her senses, making her eyes pop open. If his smile was gorgeous, his laugh was… She couldn't think of a word to describe the molten-chocolate swirl enveloping her.

'Why don't you tell me about these new experiences instead?'

Imogen opened her mouth to ask if he was really interested in hearing about them then snapped it shut.

Here was a wonderful new adventure, flirting with a gorgeous French hunk over champagne. She wasn't going to spoil it by being herself. She was going to go with the flow. This trip was about stepping out of her shell, tasting life's excitement.

Chatting with Thierry Girard was the most exciting thing that had happened to her in ages.

'I've got a list. Things I want to do.'

'In Paris?' She loved the way his eyes crinkled at the corner when he smiled.

'Not just here. I'm away from home for a month and a half but I'm only in Paris a fortnight.' She shook her head. 'I'm already realising my plans were too ambitious. I won't fit everything in.'

'That gives you a reason to return. You can do more on your next visit.'

His eyes were almost warm enough to dispel the wintry chill that descended at his words. There'd be no return visit, no second chance.

She had one shot at living to the max. She'd make the most of it, even if it meant stepping out of her comfort zone. She tossed back another mouthful of champagne, relishing the little starbursts on her tongue.

'This is delicious wine.'

He nodded. 'It's not bad. Now, tell me about this list. I'm intrigued.'

She shrugged. 'Tourist things, mainly.' But she refused to feel self-conscious. 'See those Impressionist masterpieces at the Musée d'Orsay, visit Versailles, go for a boat ride on the Seine.'

'You'll have time to fit those in if you have two weeks.'

She shook her head. 'That's only the beginning. I want to attend a gourmet cooking class. I've always wanted to know how they make those melt-in-the-mouth chocolate truffles.' The ones that were exactly the colour of his eyes.

Her breath gave a curious little hitch and she hurried on. 'I'd hoped to eat at the Eiffel Tower restaurant but I didn't realise I needed to book in advance. Plus I'd love a champagne picnic in the country and to go hot-air ballooning and drive a red convertible around the Arc de Triomphe and… Well, so many things.'

His eyebrows rose. 'Visitors are usually scared of driving there. Traffic is thick and there aren't lane markings.'

Imogen shrugged. She was scared too. But that was good. She'd feel she was really *living*.

'I like a challenge.'

'So I gather.' Was that approval in his expression? 'Have you been hot-air ballooning before?'

'Never.' She took another sip of champagne. 'This is a trip of firsts.'

'Like the champagne?' There was that delicious crinkle around his eyes. It almost lured her into believing Thierry Girard was as harmless as her work colleagues. Yet every feminine fibre screamed she was out of her depth even looking at the ultra-sexy Frenchman. Everything about him, from the breadth of his shoulders to the intriguing dark shadow across his jaw, signalled he was a virile, powerful man. 'Imogen?'

'Sorry, I was distracted.' Her voice was ridiculously husky. The way he said her name turned it into something lilting and special. She lifted her gloved fingers to her throat, as if that could ease her hammering pulse.

The glint in his eyes warned that he understood her distraction. But she refused to be embarrassed. He must be used to women going weak at the knees.

'Tell me about yourself,' she said. 'Do you live in Paris?'

He shook his head. 'Occasionally. I'm here for business meetings over the next week or two.'

'So while I'm out enjoying myself you'll be in meetings? I hope they're not too tedious.'

Nonchalantly, he lifted those impressive shoulders, and a wave of yearning washed through her. She wanted to put her hands on them, feel the strength in his tall body and lean in to see if he tasted as good as he smelled.

Imogen blinked, stunned at the force of her desire. She didn't *do* instant attraction. She didn't fall in a heap in front of any man. But her knees were suspiciously shaky and her instincts urged her to behave in ways that were completely out of character.

Was it champagne or the man? Or maybe the heady excitement of Paris and wearing Isabelle's gorgeous gown. Whatever it was, she approved. She wanted to *feel*, and from the moment her eyes had locked on Thierry's she'd felt vibrantly alive.

'You sound like you have experience of boring meetings.'

Imogen sipped more wine, enjoying the zing on her palate. 'Definitely.' She rolled her eyes. 'Our firm specialises in them. I'd bet my meetings are more boring than yours.'

'I find that hard to believe.'

Thierry took her arm and guided her away from an influx of newcomers. Even through the satin gloves his hands felt hard, capable and incredibly sexy. Trickles of fire coursed from the point of contact then splintered into incendiary darts that trailed through her body to pool down low.

How sad that she could be so turned on by that simple courteous gesture. But that wasn't surprising, given the state of her love life. Or her lack of one.

'Believe it.' She dragged herself back into the conversation. 'I'm an accountant.' She waited for his eyes to glaze over. 'A tax accountant. I know tedious.'

His lips twitched but he didn't look in the least fazed. If anything there was a spark in his gaze as it swept her from head to toe. Did it linger here and there on the way? Imogen's stomach tightened and her breasts swelled against the satin bodice as she drew a sharp breath. Strange how the lace of her strapless bra suddenly scratched at her nipples when it had been perfectly comfortable before.

'You're not acquainted with French property and commercial law, are you? The phrase "red tape" was invented to describe them. And the meetings…' He shook his head.

'You're a lawyer?' He didn't look like any lawyer she'd seen, except in some high-budget courtroom film with a smoulderingly gorgeous hero.

Thierry laughed, that rich-as-chocolate sound doing strange things to her insides. 'Me, a lawyer? That would be a match made in hell. It's bad enough being a client. My first meeting tomorrow will go all morning. I'd much rather be out of the city.'

'Really? You look like right at home here.' Her gaze skated over his hard body in that made-to-measure dinner jacket. When she lifted her eyes she found him watching her, his quirk of a smile disarming.

'This?' One casual hand gestured to his impeccable tailoring. 'This is camouflage.'

'You're saying you don't belong?' Her pulse raced at the idea of finding another outsider. For, try as she might, she couldn't feel at home in this sophisticated crowd, despite her sister's clothes.

He shrugged, and Imogen watched those wide, straight shoulders with something like hunger. She'd never felt *needy* for a man. Not even Scott. Was it this man or the unfamiliar setting that pulled her off-balance?

'I've been forced to adapt. Business means I need to be in the city. But I prefer being outdoors. There's nothing like pitting yourself against nature. It beats meetings hands-down.'

That explained those eyes. Not just the creases from sun exposure, but his deceptively lazy regard that seemed at the same time sharp and perceptive. As if from surveying distant views?

'Each hour behind a desk is pure torture.'

'You poor thing.' Impulsively, she placed her hand on his arm, then regretted it as she felt the tense and flex of sinew and impressive muscle. There it was again, that little jolt, like an electric shock. Imogen jerked her hand back, frowning, and looked at her glass. Surely she hadn't drunk enough to imagine it? Just enough to make her do something out of character, like touch a stranger.

Yet she couldn't regret it. That fierce flick of heat made her feel more alive than…

'You'd like another?' Thierry gave their glasses to a waiter and snagged two more.

She took the glass he offered, carefully avoiding contact with his tanned fingers.

'To red convertibles and champagne picnics and balloon rides.' His eyes snared hers and her heart thumped. When he looked at her, the way she imagined men looked at truly beautiful women, she almost forgot what had brought her to Paris. She could lose herself in the moment.

Imogen raised her glass. 'And to meetings that end quickly.'

'I'll drink to that.' Thierry touched his glass to hers, watching her sip her wine. She took time to taste it. Her lips, a glossy bow, pouted delectably. Her dark eyelashes quivered, and he knew she was cataloguing the prickle of bubbles on the roof of her mouth. She gave a delicate shiver of appreciation, and he found himself leaning closer.

She was so avid. So tactile. Touching her through those long gloves had made his hand tingle! From anticipation and excitement, something he usually experienced while risking his neck outdoors.

Imogen Holgate was an intriguing mix of sensuality and guilelessness.

And he wanted her.

'I can help with the ballooning.'

'Really?' Her eyes widened and he saw flecks of velvety green within the warm sherry-brown of her irises. It must be a trick of the light but her gaze seemed to glow brighter. 'That would be marvellous.'

She took a half step closer, and his breathing hitched. He inhaled the scent of vanilla sugar and warm female flesh. His taste buds tingled and his gaze dropped to her lips, then to the faint, fast pulse at her creamy throat.

He wanted to taste her, right here, now, and discover if she was as delicious as he expected. He wanted to sweep her to some place where he could learn her secrets.

Hazel eyes and vanilla sugar as an aphrodisiac?

His tastes had changed. She was completely different from Sandrine and all the women since her. Yet sexual hunger honed his senses to a keen edge. He searched out the nearest exit, the part of his brain that was pure hunter planning how to cut her from the crowd when the time was ripe.

'I'd appreciate it if you could.' Her words interrupted his thoughts, or maybe it was that excited smile making her face glow. 'I should have researched it earlier but this trip was on the spur of the moment. Can you recommend a company I could contact?'

It took longer than it should have to remember what they were talking about. 'Better than that. A friend runs a balloon company outside Paris. We used to make balloon treks together.'

'Really?' Her eyes widened and there again was that trick of the light, for they seemed almost pure green now. How would they look when ecstasy took her? The tension in his lower body ratcheted up too many notches for comfort. 'You've been ballooning? Tell me all about it. Please?'

She clutched his arm and that shimmer of sensation rippled up it.

Over the next twenty minutes she peppered him with questions. Not the usual *What's it like up there?* and *Aren't you afraid of falling?* but everything from safety procedures to the amount of fuel required, from measuring height to landing procedure. All the while her expression kept shifting. He didn't know whether he preferred her serious, poutingly curious or dreamy-eyed excited.

She was enchanting. Refreshingly straightforward, yet complex and intriguing. And passionate.

He watched her lips as she spoke and desire exploded.

How long since he'd felt like this?

How long since he'd met a woman fascinated by him and his interest in adventure rather than money, social status or his reputation as a lover?

Plus she was passing through. She'd have no aspirations to tie him down.

Imogen was the perfect short-term diversion.

CHAPTER TWO

THE LIGHTS DIMMED and at the far end of the room a band struck up. The swell of the bass was incongruous in this ornate setting, but no one seemed surprised, even when beams of purple, blue and white light shot across the crowd.

A spotlight caught Imogen's eyes and she flinched, moving closer to Thierry. Instantly, his arm curved protectively around her. She liked that too much, but she had no desire to pull away. Not when every nerve screamed at her to lean into him.

His arm was hard and reassuring as the band's volume rose to a pounding beat. Imogen relished the unfamiliar thrill of being close to all that imposing masculinity. For, despite his perfectly tailored suit, there was no disguising that Thierry was all hard-muscled man.

His hands were a giveaway too. Neat, clean nails, but there were tiny, pale scars across his tanned skin, hinting he did more than wield a pen.

Imogen wondered how they'd feel on her bare flesh.

He said something she didn't hear over a crescendo of music. At the same time the light show became more frenetic, a staccato pulse in time with the drums. Imogen felt it all swirl and coalesce like a living thing. Light stabbed her eyes.

Not now. Please not now!

Just a little more time. Was that too much to ask?

Her stomach cramped and her breathing jammed. She blinked. It wasn't the light from the stage blinding her, it was the white-hot knife jabbing inside her skull. Her vision blurred, pain sawing through her.

'Imogen?' That arm at her back tightened. She caught

a drift of something in her nostrils, some essence that reminded her of the outdoors, before the metallic taste of pain obliterated everything. Sheer willpower kept her on her feet, knees desperately locked.

'I…' It came out as a whisper. She tried again. 'I'd like to leave.'

'Of course.' He took the glass from her unresisting hand. 'This way.' He turned her towards the exit but she stumbled, her legs not obeying.

Music shuddered through her, a screaming beat, and in her head the jab, jab, jab of that unseen knife.

Warmth engulfed her and it took a moment to realise it was from Thierry's powerful body as he wrapped his arm around her waist and half carried her from the room.

Imagine what he could do with two arms.

And those hands. You've always had a thing for great hands.

That was her last coherent thought till they were in the peace of an anteroom. She couldn't recall exactly how he'd got her there but the lean strength of his body made her feel anchored and safe, despite the lancing pain.

'Imogen? What is it? Talk to me.' His accent was more pronounced, slurring the words sexily. Even in her dazed state she heard his concern.

'Headache. Sorry.' She tilted her head up, trying to bring him into focus through slitted yes.

'A migraine?' Gently, he pulled her to him, resting her head on his shoulder and palming her hair in a rhythmic touch that amazingly seemed to make the pain recede a little.

She wanted never to move, just sink into his calm strength. The realisation she'd never be held like this again by anyone brought a sob rushing to her throat. She stifled it. Pity wouldn't help.

'Sorry.' She sucked air through clenched teeth as she straightened. 'Enjoy the rest of the party. It's been—'

'Where are you staying?' His voice was low, soothing.

'Here. Three-hundred and five.' She fumbled in her purse, dragging out her key card. All she had to do was get to her room.

Had he read her befuddled mind? One minute she stood on trembling legs, the next she was swept up in his embrace. She felt bone and muscle, the tickle of his breath on her face. She should have objected. Breathing through excruciating pain, she merely slumped against him, grateful that for once she didn't have to manage alone.

This past year she'd had to be strong, for her mother and more recently for herself. Leaning against Thierry, feeling the steady thud of his heart beneath his jacket, she felt a little of the tightness racking her body ease. Was it her imagination or did the pain pull back a fraction? She shut her eyes, focusing on his iron-hard arms beneath her, the comfort of his embrace.

Another first. Being swept off your feet by a man.

Warm fingers touched hers as he shifted his hold and took the card from her hand.

'Here we are.' His deep voice wrapped around her. 'Not long now.' A door snicked closed and soon she was lowered onto a mattress. Smoothly, without hesitation, his hands withdrew and Imogen knew a moment's craziness when she had to bite back a plea that he not let her go. There'd been such comfort in being held.

Her eyes shot open and she winced, even in the soft glow from a single bedside lamp. Thierry towered above her, concern lining his brow.

'What do you need? Painkillers? Water?'

Gingerly, she moved, the smallest of nods. 'Water, please.' While he got it she fumbled open her bedside drawer and took out her medication with a shaking hand.

'Let me.' He squatted, popped the tablet and handed it to her. Then he raised her head while she swallowed it and sipped the water, his touch sure but gentle. Stupidly, tears clung to her lashes. Tears for this stranger's tenderness. Tears for the extravagant fantasy she'd dared harbour, of ending the night in Thierry's arms, making love with this sexy, fascinating, gorgeous man.

Fantasy wasn't for her. Her reality was too stark for that. She'd have to make do with scraping whatever small pleasures she could from life before it was too late.

Defeated, she slumped against the pillow, forcing herself to meet his concerned gaze.

'You're very kind. Thank you, Thierry. I can manage from here.'

Kind be damned. He looked into drowning eyes shimmering green and golden-brown and his belly twisted. This woman had hooked him with her vibrancy, humour and enthusiasm, not to mention her flagrant sexiness. Even her slight hesitancy over his name appealed ridiculously. Her vulnerability was a punch to the gut, and not just because he'd aimed to spend the night with her.

'Shut your eyes and relax.'

'I will.'

As soon as you leave. The unspoken words hung between them and who could blame her? He was a virtual stranger. Except he felt curiously like he'd known her half his life or, more correctly, had waited that long to meet her.

A frisson of warning ripped through him but he ignored it. She was no threat. With her tear-spiked lashes and too-pale face, she was the picture of vulnerability. There were shadows beneath her eyes too that he hadn't seen before.

'What are you doing?' Her voice was husky, doing dangerous things to his body. Thierry had to remind himself it was from pain, not arousal.

He put the house phone to his ear, dialling room service. 'Getting you peppermint tea. My *grand-mère* suffers from migraines and that helps.'

'That's kind but…' Her words petered out as he ordered the tea then replaced the phone.

'Just try it, okay? If it doesn't work you can leave it.' He straightened and stepped back, putting distance between them. 'I'll stay till it's delivered so you don't have to get up.'

She opened her mouth then shut it, surveying him with pain-clouded eyes. Again that stab to his gut. He frowned and turned towards the bathroom, speaking over his shoulder. 'You're safe with me, Imogen. I have no ulterior motives.' *Not now, at any rate*. 'Trust me. I was a Boy Scout, did I tell you?'

When he returned with a damp flannel, he caught the wry twist of her lips.

'I'm to trust you because you were a Boy Scout?' Her voice was pain-roughened but there was that note of almost-laughter he'd found so attractive earlier.

'Of course. Ready to serve and always prepared.' He brushed back a few escaped locks of hair and placed the flannel on her forehead.

She sighed, and he made himself retreat rather than trace that glossy, silk-soft hair again. He pulled up a chair and sat a couple of metres from the bed.

Shimmering, half-lidded eyes met his. 'Are all Frenchmen so take-charge?'

'Are all Australian women so obstinate?'

A tiny smile curved her lips, and she shut her eyes. Ridiculously that smile felt like a victory.

The musical chimes of a mobile phone grew louder, drawing the attention of other café patrons. It was only then that Imogen realised it was her phone chirping away in her bag. In a fit of out-with-the-old-Imogen energy, she'd decided the old, plain ring tone was boring, swapping it for a bright pop tune.

'Hello?'

'Imogen?' His voice was smooth and warm, deep enough to make her shiver.

'Thierry?' The word was a croak of surprise. She'd berated herself all morning for wishing last night hadn't ended the way it had.

The fact Thierry had stayed so long only showed how dreadful she must have looked. And that he was what her mum would have called 'a true gentleman'.

'How are you today? Are you feeling better?'

'Good, thank you. I'm fit as a fiddle.' An exaggeration—those headaches always left her wrung out. But she was perking up by the moment. 'How are you?'

There was a crack of laughter, and Imogen's hand tightened on the phone. Even from a distance his laugh melted something inside. She sank back in her chair, noticing for the first time a blue patch of sky through the grey cloud.

'All the better for hearing your voice.'

She blinked, registering his deep, seductive tone. Her blood pumped faster and she tried to tell herself she imagined it. Nothing, she knew, put men off as much as illness. Even illness by proxy. For a moment Scott's face swam in her vision till she banished it.

'How did you get my number?'

There was a moment's silence. 'Your mobile was on the bedside table last night.'

'You took the number down?'

'You're annoyed?'

Annoyed? 'No. Not at all.' Surprised. Delighted. *Excited!* A little buzz of pleasure zoomed through her.

As she watched, the blue patch of sky grew and a beam of sunlight glanced down on the wet cobblestones, making them gleam. The café door opened behind her and the delicious aroma of fresh coffee drifted out.

'What's on your agenda this evening? Night-time bungee jumping? Motorcycle lessons? Or maybe that ghost tour?'

She smiled, enjoying his teasing. 'I'm still deciding between a couple of options.' Like a long bubble bath, painting her nails scarlet or gathering her courage and finding the dance venue Saskia had mentioned.

'How would you like dinner at the Eiffel Tower? There's an unexpected vacancy.'

'There is?' She sat up. 'But I couldn't get a reservation when I tried.'

'There's one for you now if you want it.'

'Of course I want it!' She squashed a howl of disappointment at the idea of dining in such a romantic setting alone. But she was a pragmatist. She'd learned to face hard truths. Thierry felt sorry for her after last night and had arranged this treat. 'It was kind of you to do that, Thierry. Thank you.'

'Excellent. I'll collect you at eight.'

'Eight?' She blinked, dazed. He was collecting her? He was taking her to dinner?

'Yes. See you then.'

He ended the call, and Imogen stared at the phone. Thierry Girard, the most drool-worthy, fascinating, charming man she'd ever met, was taking her to dinner? She didn't know whether to be stunned or nervous.

She settled for thrilled.

Imogen felt like she floated on air as they drove back to her hotel. The evening had been perfect. The food, the wine, the company, the weight of Thierry's gaze on her like a touch.

When he surveyed the dress of green and bronze her sister Izzy had created, his eyes lingered appreciatively. But when his attention roved again and again to Imogen's bare throat and shoulders, and especially her lips, heat coiled inside, like a clock wound too tight.

It made her laughter at his outrageous stories die, replaced by a hunger that no food could remedy. Was it possible to explode with sheer longing for a man's touch?

Did she have the nerve to follow through? Casual sex wasn't in her repertoire. Yet there was nothing casual about how Thierry made her feel.

The question was, what did he feel? Was tonight a random kindness to a stranger or something else? Imogen wished she knew. She had absolutely no experience of high-octane, sophisticated men like Thierry Girard.

He stopped the car before her hotel and she turned towards him, only to find he was already out the door, striding around the car. A moment later her door swung open and he was helping her out.

Now. Ask him now before he says goodnight.

But her throat jammed as he hooked her hand over his arm and led her into the grand hotel—her big splurge on this end-of-a-lifetime trip. His heat, his scent, fresh as the outdoors, and the feel of his body against hers, made her light-headed. He led her through the luxurious foyer, past staff who stopped to greet them, to the bank of lifts.

'I—' Her words died as he stepped into the lift with her and hit the button for her floor.

So, he was seeing her to her room. She shot him a sideways look, discovering that in profile his features were taut, as if his earlier good humour had faded.

Abruptly, her anticipation drained away.

Had she misread him? Perhaps he didn't feel that hum of sexual arousal, that edge-of-seat excitement. Maybe he'd used up all his charm entertaining the unsophisticated tourist over dinner. She'd known last night she was out of place at that glamorous party, despite the wonderful dress she wore. Maybe after hours in her company he'd realised it too. Did he regret asking her out?

'You…?' Eyes of ebony locked with hers, and she sagged in Izzy's green stilettos.

Izzy would have known what to say. How to entertain

and attract him and, above all, follow through. Imogen's only intimate experience had been with Scott, cautious Scott, who never acted on impulse, never broke rules or took a chance. He'd never made her feel the way Thierry did.

But, cataloguing the tension in her companion's shoulders and the pronounced angle of his strong jaw, she realised her mistake. Thierry's was a casual charm. Of course he didn't want more from her. He was French. He was being polite. And those heavy-lidded looks that stopped her breath? They probably came naturally to him and didn't mean anything.

'It's kind of you to see me to my room.'

The doors slid open, and he ushered her down the hall to her room, her arm clamped to his side.

Probably afraid you'll collapse like you did last night.

'That's the second time you've accused me of being kind.' His voice sounded tight, but she didn't look at him, delving instead into her purse for her key card.

'You've been wonderful, and I appreciate it. I—' She frowned as he took the card and opened the door.

Did he have to be so eager to say goodnight?

But, instead of saying goodbye, Thierry stepped over the threshold, drawing her in. The door closed behind them and, stunned, Imogen turned. His tanned features looked chiselled, uncompromising, and those liquid, dark eyes…

'I'm not good at "kind".' He stroked a finger down her cheek in a barely there touch that rocketed to the centre of her being. 'In fact, I excel at doing exactly what pleases me most.' His head dipped, and Imogen's breath stalled as his breath caressed her lips. 'And what pleases me most is to be with you, Imogen.'

Imogen swallowed hard. It was what she wanted, what she'd steeled herself to ask. Yet part of her, the cautious, reserved part that had kept her safe for twenty-five years, froze her tongue.

Safe? There was no safe, not any more. Not when she could count the future in months, not decades.

'Or am I wrong?' His hand dropped, and still she felt his touch like a sense memory. 'Do you not want…?'

'Yes!' Her purse tumbled to the floor as her hand shot out. She clutched his fingers, threading hers through them. The flash of heat from the contact point was like an electric charge. 'I want.'

How badly she wanted. Need was a shimmering wave, engulfing her.

He didn't smile. If anything his features grew harder, flesh pulling taut across those magnificent bones. His fingers tightened around hers.

'I can offer you short-term pleasure, Imogen. That's all.' His eyes narrowed as if he tried to read her thoughts. 'If that's not what you want—'

Her finger on his mouth stopped his words and sent another ripple of sensual awareness through her. Despite his honed, masculine features his lips were surprisingly soft. She felt light-headed just thinking about them on her mouth.

'That sounds perfect.' She drew a breath shaky with grim amusement. 'I'm not in the market for long term.'

The words were barely out when his head swooped and his mouth met hers. Firmly, implacably, no teasing, just the sure, sensual demand of a man who knew what he wanted and, Imogen realised as her lips parted, who knew how to please a woman. The swipe of his tongue, the angle of his mouth, the possessive clasp of his hand around her skull were so *right*; she wondered how she'd gone her whole life without experiencing anything like it.

Whatever she and Scott had shared, it was nothing like this.

Thierry circled an arm around her, pulling her against his hard frame. Everywhere they touched, from her breasts to her thighs, exploded into tingling awareness, as if she'd brushed a live wire. Darts of fire shot to her nipples, her pelvis, even up the back of her neck as he massaged her scalp, and she heard herself moan into his mouth.

He tasted better than chocolate, rich, strong and addictive. She slid her arms around his neck and hung on tight as her knees gave way.

Instantly, the arm at her back tightened. He swung her off the ground, high in his arms, making her feel precious and feminine against his imposing masculinity. His mouth devoured hers, seeking, demanding, yet giving so much pleasure that exultation filled her.

This was a kiss. *This* was desire.

She was greedy for him, hungry for the passion he'd stoked so easily. She pushed her fingers through his hair, its soft thickness enticing.

'More,' she mumbled against his lips.

For answer she felt movement. Then she was on the bed and he over her, his weight pressing her down, his long legs imprisoning hers. She'd never felt anything as erotic as his hard length pinioning her, his breath hot on her neck as he grazed her with his teeth, making her jolt and squirm.

'Thierry!' That scraping little nip at the spot where her neck met her shoulders had her shuddering as great looping waves of delight coursed through her. They swamped her body, arrowing in to concentrate at the sensitive point between her legs.

He shifted his weight, settling low in the cradle of her hips, and she throbbed deep inside.

Urgently, Imogen arched, feeling the strong column of his arousal between her legs, and her brain shorted. She slid her hand down, wrapping around the solid weight of him, needing that contact. Desperate for more.

His breath hissed as he lifted his head. One large hand covered hers, holding her palm against him for a moment then dragging it away.

'Patience, Imogen.' She barely comprehended. His accent was so thick and her ears so full of her pulse pounding like the thud of a hammer on metal.

'Yes, now.' Was that reedy, desperate voice hers?

His eyes looked smoky, on the edge of focus, as he forced her arm wide, imprisoning her hand. When she shifted and brought her other hand down to touch him he pulled that arm wide too, so she lay spread-eagled.

The action pressed his groin against her pelvis, and her eyelids fluttered. Circling her hips, she moved against him, and to her amazement almost tipped over the edge into ecstasy. How could pleasure be so intense? So instantaneous? With Scott…

Thought died as Thierry murmured something in that lush, deep voice and lowered his head again. His breath feathered the sensitive flesh of her neck and then warm lips pressed just there and… Oh, yes, just there.

Again that powerful pulse through her pelvis, making every muscle clench and every erogenous zone shiver in anticipation.

'No. Don't!' It was a gurgle of sound, a hoarse whisper scraped from the back of her throat, but he heard it. Stilled.

She felt him draw a deep breath, his chest expanding. His hands tightened as if in spasm before loosing their hold. Then he pulled back, lifting his head.

Gone was the urbane sophisticate. Gone was the man in control. The glittering eyes that met hers held an unfamiliar wildness. His lips were a twist of what looked like raw pain.

Imogen watched him open his mouth. He shut his eyes and swallowed. Fascinated, she followed the jerky movement of his throat. Then blazing, dark eyes met hers again. 'You've changed your mind?' Even his voice was unfamiliar.

'Of course not.' How could he even think it? 'But I can't wait. I need you *now*.' Already she was running her hands over him, revelling in the heat of ridged muscle beneath his fine shirt. One hand dipped to his belt buckle and her fingers fumbled in their haste.

Thierry's eyes widened, his body rigid, as if he couldn't trust her words. Hadn't he ever met a woman so eager for him? Impossible!

What was impossible was that she, Imogen Holgate, was so desperate she didn't think she'd survive another minute of his seduction.

He was going to kiss and caress her, taking his time, and she'd self-combust at any moment. She'd never known anything like this spike of arousal.

'Please, Thierry.' Finally, she got his buckle undone and slid the belt free with clumsy hands. 'You can seduce me later. Whatever you like. But I need you inside me now.'

Fire washed from her throat to her hairline. But she didn't care about embarrassment or appearing unsophisticated. *Desire* was too tame a word for this urgent, visceral need. Nothing mattered but being one with this man.

Imogen bit her lip as her fingers slipped on his zip. She tried again and heard his sharp inhale. Hard fingers closed around hers.

He wasn't going to stop her, was he? Not now. She almost sobbed with frustration, her whole body burning like a single, vibrant flame that would at any minute consume her.

'Let me, *ma chérie*.'

Thierry kept his eyes on her face as he shucked his shoes and grabbed one of the condoms he'd brought.

She was glorious, her skin flushed with sexual arousal. Her eyes were bright as stars, veiled by long black lashes. Her reddened lips were plump and inviting, but not as inviting as the rest of her. His movements quickened, sheathing himself as his gaze dropped to proud breasts straining against that tight bodice. A surge of hunger hit and he drew an uneven breath. Despite what she said he needed to rein himself in, not surrender to hunger and take her with no preliminaries. He needed to…

Thierry's thoughts spun away as she reefed up the hem of her dress. Long, pale, toned thighs. Skimpy, emerald-green lace panties. The subtle, enticing scent of vanilla sugar and feminine arousal.

Slender fingers hooked the green lace and she arched her hips up, wriggling, to pull it away.

His hands tangled with hers, stripping the lace off. Then his hands were on her, skimming satin-soft flesh, stroking the dark silk, already damp, at her core.

He didn't register moving closer. But an instant later he was there, pressing against her softness, his hands planted beside her on the bed. Her skirt was up around her waist and her hair had come down on one side, dark tresses curling to her breasts.

A shudder ripped through him. He wanted to feast on her, take his time to build their pleasure, but he couldn't.

It wasn't the tug of her fingers digging into his shoulders that shattered his control, or the tiny, throaty purring sound she made. It was simply that he'd never wanted a woman so urgently.

His hand shook as he lifted her to him. Then in one sure, glorious stroke he surged home, high and hard, till he felt nothing but her, knew nothing but her liquid heat, sweet scent and indescribable pleasure.

Tawny green eyes snared his. Her head pressed back, baring that delectable throat. He heard his name in a throaty, broken gasp. It was the sexiest thing he'd ever heard, and to his amazement was all it took for him to lose the last of his control.

She quivered, jerking and shaking around him, drawing him into the most mind-blowing climax he'd ever experienced.

It was a long, long time before his brain functioned again. Imogen shifted drowsily, and he found himself quickening into arousal again. His immediate thought was to wonder if he'd brought enough condoms.

His second, when her eyes fluttered open and her tentative smile hit him square in the chest, was to congratulate himself on finding her. He'd never known a woman so unstinting in her passion.

Two weeks would barely be enough to enjoy all she had to offer. Yet that was all they had. She'd be gone in a fortnight.

Thierry felt a flicker of something almost like regret. But it would dissipate. A temporary lover was all he wanted. A couple of months and he'd be free of the shackles that had tied him down for four years. Then he'd leave, ready for adventure and the physical and mental challenges he missed. Which was why Imogen, who could only ever be temporary in his life, was absolutely perfect.

CHAPTER THREE

IMOGEN STARED FROM her hotel window at the London square with its communal garden and neat Georgian buildings. A couple strolled by hand in hand and her stomach did a little somersault. She looked away, lifting her peppermint tea to her lips.

She'd developed a taste for herbal tea since that night in Paris when Thierry had ordered it for her.

Turning, she found her gaze following the couple and felt a pang of regret. They were in their seventies, she'd guess, yet they held hands, heads turned towards each other as if in conversation.

What would it be like to grow old with the man you loved? The question wormed into her brain and she had to slam down a protective portcullis before her thoughts went too far.

Thierry Girard had been a revelation. Any woman would have been in heaven experiencing Paris with him, even if she hadn't spent years buried in a half-life of tedium, hemmed in by caution. Was it any wonder Venice, Reykjavik and London hadn't seemed quite as fabulous as Paris? He'd brought the city alive.

He'd brought *her* alive.

But she couldn't give in to romantic fantasy.

What they'd had had been wonderful and she'd lingered over each memory, loving the hazy sense of wellbeing they brought. But their passion, the romance and sense of connection had been illusory, the product of an affair that could only be short-lived.

She sipped her tea then grimaced as her taste buds did that strange thing again, turning a flavour she enjoyed into a dull, metallic tang. She put the cup down then realised she'd turned too fast, for the nausea rose again. Imogen gripped the table, taking slow breaths.

Her mother hadn't had these symptoms. Did it mean Imogen's condition was different after all? If anything the headaches had eased a little and were less frequent. But the nausea worried her. It was so persistent.

Reluctantly, she turned towards the bathroom. It was silly to consider the possibility of it being anything else. There was no chance a woman in her condition…

She shook her head then regretted it as the movement stirred that sick feeling again.

Clamping her lips, she headed to the bathroom. Of course it was absurd. This must be a new symptom of her deteriorating condition. Though, with the exception of the nausea, she felt better than she had in ages.

What was the point of second-guessing? She needed to see the specialist back in Sydney. He'd explain what was happening. How long she had.

Imogen drew a slow breath, deliberately pushing her shoulders down as tension inched them higher. Whatever the future held, she'd meet it head on.

She crossed the bathroom and reached for the test kit she'd left there. She hadn't had the nerve to look at the result before, telling herself it was nonsense and she'd be better having tea and biscuits to settle her stomach.

Now, reluctantly, she looked down at the indicator.

The world wobbled and she grabbed the counter.

Had her illness affected her eyes? But the indicator was clear. It was only her brain that felt blurry.

Pregnant.

She was expecting Thierry's child.

It was harder, this time, to contact him. He had a new PA who seemed dauntingly efficient and not eager to help.

No, Monsieur Girard wasn't in Paris. No, she couldn't

say where he was. Her tone implied Imogen had no right to renew his acquaintance. Had she been placed on some blacklist of importunate ex-lovers? Imogen imagined a throng of women trailing after him, trying to recapture his attention.

Was she to be so easily dismissed? Embarrassment and anger warred, and her grip tightened on the phone.

'When will he be back? It's urgent I speak with him.' She'd taken the first train from London to Paris, checking into a tiny hotel with the last of her travel money.

'Perhaps you'd like to leave a message, *mademoiselle*? He's very busy.' The cool tone implied he'd never find time for her again. Was that an overprotective assistant or a woman acting on orders?

Her crisp efficiency and Imogen's realisation she could only contact him via this dragon brought home the glaring differences between them. Thierry was powerful, mixing in elite social circles and living a privileged life. Employees protected him from unsolicited contact. She was working class and unsophisticated, more at home with a spreadsheet of numbers than at a glittering social event. Only the bright passion between them had made them equals.

Imogen set her chin.

'I need to speak with him in person. It's imperative.'

'As I said, I can take a message…'

But would it be delivered?

Imogen gritted her teeth, staring over the slate-grey roof of the building across the lane. It seemed close enough to touch in this cheap back street. A far cry from the magnificent hotel she'd splurged on during her first stay in Paris.

'Please tell him I need to see him. Five minutes will do.' She bit down grim laughter. How long did it take to break such news? 'I have…important information for him. Something he needs to hear as soon as possible.'

'Very well, *mademoiselle*.' The phone clicked in her ear.

* * *

'That's all now.' Thierry looked at his watch. 'Finish those in the morning.'

Mademoiselle Janvier primmed her mouth. 'I find it more efficient to complete my work before leaving and start fresh tomorrow.'

Thierry forbore from comment. His temporary PA took efficiency to a new level. At least these notes would take no more than half an hour.

He should be grateful. When there'd been that recent glitch in his plans to take over a rival business, her hard work had been invaluable. She'd even tried to match his eighteen-hour work days till he'd put a stop to it. Dedication he appreciated, but sometimes she seemed almost *proprietorial*.

If only she'd smile occasionally.

His lips twitched. That was his unregenerate, unbusinesslike side. The side that preferred being outdoors on a clear evening like this, rather than cooped up with a sour-faced assistant.

That part of him would far rather share a champagne picnic with an intriguing dark-haired beauty whose enthusiasm, sensuality and unexpected flashes of naïveté intrigued.

That couldn't be regret he felt? There'd be excitement enough in his life once he cleared this final hurdle. He'd given up four years of his life and wrought a small miracle, wresting the family business from the brink of disaster. Soon…

He rolled his shoulders. Soon he could take up his real life again. The one that defined him, no matter how irresponsible his *grand-père* branded it. But his *grand-père* had never understood it was the rush of adrenalin, the thrill of pitting himself physically against the toughest challenges, that made him feel *real*. These past years he'd been condemned to a half life.

Adventure beckoned. What would it be first? Heli-skiing or hot-air ballooning? Or white-water rafting? Orsino had mentioned a place in Colorado…

'By the way, there's a woman waiting to see you.'

'A woman?' Thierry checked his diary. He had no appointments.

'A Mademoiselle Holgate.'

'Holgate?' Something inside his chest jerked hard. 'How long has she been waiting?'

His PA's eyes widened as he shot to his feet. 'I warned her she'd have to wait. You had a lot—'

'Invite her in. Immediately!'

Mademoiselle Janvier scurried out, shock on her thin features. It was the first time she'd seen him anything but polite and calm, even when it had looked like his expansion plans, so vital to the solidity of the company, had unravelled.

The door opened and his breathing quickened. He stepped around the desk, elation pulsing.

Elation? He halted, a prickle of warning skating through him.

He and Imogen had enjoyed themselves but Thierry wasn't in the habit of feeling more than casual pleasure at the thought of any woman. Not since Sandrine, a lifetime ago.

He'd learned his lesson then. Women added spice and pleasure, especially now his chance for serious adventure had been curtailed. But none lasted. He made sure of it. Women fitted into the category of rest and recreation.

Thierry frowned as a trim, dark-haired figure stepped into the room and an unfamiliar sensation clamped his belly.

He almost wouldn't have recognised her. Those glorious dark tresses were scraped into a bun that reminded him of Mademoiselle Janvier with her rigid self-control. Imogen wore jeans and a shirt that leached the colour from her face. He'd never seen her in anything but bright colours. And there were shadows under her eyes, hollows beneath her cheekbones.

Again that inexplicable thump to his chest, as if an unseen hand had punched him.

'Imogen!' He started forward but before he reached her she slipped into a visitor's chair.

Thierry pulled up abruptly. It wasn't the reaction he got from women. Ever.

'Thierry.' She nodded, the movement curt, almost dismissive. And her eyes—they didn't glow as he remembered. They looked…haunted as they stared at his tie. Yet there was defiance in the set of her chin. Belligerence in her clamped lips.

What had happened? He'd seen her ecstatic, curious, enthralled. He'd seen her in the throes of passion. His lower body tensed. Those memories had kept him from sleep too many nights since she'd left. He'd even seen her in pain, with tears spiking those ebony lashes. But he'd never seen her look like this.

He grabbed a chair, yanked it around to face her and sank onto it, his knees all but touching her thighs.

She shifted, pulling her legs away, as if he made her nervous. Or as if his touch contaminated.

Something jabbed his gut. Deliberately, he leaned back, gaze bland, his mind buzzing with questions.

'This is an unexpected pleasure.'

'Is it? That's not the impression I got.' Her chin lifted infinitesimally and colour swept her too-pale face. That was better. The woman he knew had sass and vibrancy.

'You've just walked in the door.' He gave her the smile he knew melted female hearts. Despite her tension it was good to see her. He'd missed her more than he'd expected and—

'I suppose I should be grateful you found time out of your busy schedule to see me.'

* * *

Imogen bit her lip. This wasn't going right. She'd let fear and anger get the best of her. Anger at how long it had taken to see him, only then to be kept waiting for an hour. And fear. Fear that even with his help, assuming he would help her, the new life growing inside her was likely in danger.

She threaded her fingers together, trying to hide their tremor.

It didn't help that one glance was all she'd needed to fall under Thierry's spell again. He looked wonderful. Strong and fit, so utterly masculine that just sitting beside him was a test of endurance. She wanted to touch him, feel that strong life-force, remind herself there was some hope in this bleak situation.

'I'm sorry you had to wait. I didn't know you were there.'

Imogen waved a dismissive hand, her gaze skating across the huge office with its expansive, and expensive, views over one of Paris's most prestigious neighbourhoods.

'It doesn't matter.' She drew a breath, trying to slow her racing heart, only to discover she'd inhaled his distinctive scent—warm male flesh and clear mountain air. It teased her nostrils and set up a trembling deep inside.

For one self-indulgent instant she let herself remember how glorious it had been between them. How perfect.

But that was over. He'd moved on and she, well, she had more important things to worry about than her attraction to a heartbreaker of a Frenchman.

'I thought you'd be in Australia now. Wasn't it Venice, Reykjavik, London and then home to Sydney?'

He remembered. A tiny curl of delight swirled inside. 'That was the plan.' Her voice emerged husky, not like the firm tone she'd aimed for. 'But things have changed.'

'I'm glad.' His voice caressed. 'I've been thinking of you.'

Surprised, she jerked her head up, their eyes meeting.

Instantly, sultry heat unfurled in her belly like coiling tendrils. Her skin drew taut.

She didn't know how Thierry did that. She didn't know whether to be shocked, stoic or despairing that absence hadn't lessened his impact. Even with so much on her mind, that low voice, that slurred ripple of accented sound, made her body hum.

He leaned close, and she sat back, seeing the moment he registered her withdrawal. A frown puckered his brow.

'I came because I had some news.'

He stilled, and she sensed a watchfulness that belied his air of unconcern.

When they'd been together all that powerful energy had been focused on pleasure. Now, in this vast office that screamed authority, with those unblinking eyes trained on her, she saw how formidable Thierry was. Not just as the sexiest, most charismatic man she'd ever met, but because of the power he wielded with such ease.

She swallowed, her throat suddenly parched.

'News?' The word was sharp.

'Yes.' She swiped her top lip with her tongue and a flicker of something crossed his proud features. 'Yes, I…'

Spit it out! How hard is it to say? You've had a week of waiting to get used to it.

'You…?' He leaned forward, and she knew an urge to slide onto his lap and burrow close.

As if Thierry's embrace would make everything right! *Nothing* could make this right.

Again she licked her lips. 'I'm pregnant.'

For what seemed a full minute he said nothing, merely looked at her with a face frozen into harsh lines that emphasised the chiselled hauteur of those superb features.

'You say the baby is mine?'

Mistake number one, Thierry realised when Imogen snapped back in her seat as if yanked by a bungee cord.

Ice formed in her hazel eyes, turning them from warm and a little lost to frozen wasteland. Then there was the taut line of her mouth, the hurt in the way she bit her lip.

He hated it when she did that. He always wanted to reach out and stop her. And she…

Belatedly, he yanked back his thoughts. Pregnant. With his child?

His breath disintegrated and a sense of unreality engulfed him. Like the day, as a kid, when he'd learned his parents had died in a crash outside Lyon. Or four years ago, when his indomitable *grand-père* had had a stroke.

Was it possible?

Of course it was possible. He and Imogen had spent every night for almost two weeks together, insatiable for each other.

He'd never known any woman to test his control the way Imogen had. He'd plan some outing to tick off her bucket list—a visit to a dance club, or a moonlight picnic—and all the time she was beaming at him, laughing and thrilled at the novelty of new experiences, he was calculating how long before he could get her naked and horizontal. Or just naked enough for sex. As for horizontal…the missionary position was overrated.

Molten heat coiled in his belly.

'There's been no one else. Just you.'

Stupid to feel that punch of pleasure. Thierry forced himself to focus. This was too important.

'Since when?'

'That's not relevant. I—'

'Since when, Imogen?' Stranger things had happened than a woman trying to pin an unexpected pregnancy on some gullible man.

Her chin rose and the expression in her eyes could have scored flesh. 'Seven months.'

So long between lovers? Did that make him special, or a convenient way of ending the drought? Or maybe a target?

'That's very precise.'

'I don't make a habit of sleeping around.'

He'd worked it out. He vividly recalled her charmingly unpractised loving, the shock in her eyes at the ecstasy they'd shared.

'Pregnant.' He paused, frustrated that his brain wouldn't function. Now it had side-tracked into imagining Imogen swollen with his child, her hands splayed over her ripe belly. He'd never lusted after a pregnant woman yet the image in his head filled him with all sorts of inappropriate thoughts.

Diable! He should be concentrating, not mentally undressing her.

He dragged his attention back to her face. 'We used condoms.'

Jerkily she nodded. 'It turns out they're not a hundred percent effective.'

'You're sure about this?' He searched her features. She looked different—drawn and tired. And…was that fear?

'I wouldn't be here if I weren't. I took the test in London. That's why I came to Paris, to find you.'

Thierry stared into those haunted eyes and told himself the sensible thing would be to insist on a paternity test. He had only her word the child was his.

Yet, crazy as it was, he was on the verge of believing her. He'd been with her just two weeks, but he felt he knew her better than any of the women he'd dated.

Even better than Sandrine.

The thought sideswiped him. He'd grown up with Sandrine and had loved her with all his youthful heart.

The memory served its purpose, like being doused in a cold mountain stream. He needed to think critically. He straightened.

'What sort of test was it? One from a pharmacy?'

She nodded. 'That's right.'

Thierry stood, relieved to have a purpose. He strode

around the desk and reached for a phone. 'Then the first thing to do is get this confirmed by a doctor.'

The flare of relief in Imogen's eyes intrigued him. She didn't look like a woman trying to catch a man by getting pregnant.

She looked scared rigid.

'Well, that settles that.' Thierry's voice was as delicious as ever, the silky burr a ribbon of warmth threading Imogen's ice-cold body as they left the doctor's rooms.

She'd felt chilled and resentful all through the consultation. Perhaps because Thierry had insisted he remain, as if he didn't trust her. Perhaps from embarrassment, because she couldn't shake the idea the doctor, for all his professionalism, was quietly judging her and sympathising with Thierry. He'd continually addressed Thierry rather than her. As if she didn't have the wit to comprehend her condition.

Or as if she was an inconvenient problem.

'What does it settle?'

Thierry didn't answer. She darted him a sideways stare and guessed he was brooding over his own thoughts. That wide brow was furrowed, his eyes focused on the glistening cobblestones as they walked.

Yet, distracted as he was, his hand was reassuring in the small of her back. It felt...protective.

Imogen was needy enough right now to appreciate that.

Since the realisation of her fatal condition, she'd felt separated from the world by a wall of glass. Only her brief time with Thierry had seemed *real*. But the news she was pregnant... She'd never felt so frighteningly alone in all her life. Being responsible for another life as she faced the end of her own—how was she going to manage it?

She stumbled, and Thierry's arm slid around her waist, holding her upright and safe. She stopped, her heart hammering high in her throat.

What if she'd fallen? Would such a simple tumble be enough to dislodge that tiny life? Surely not? Yet Imogen's palm crept to her abdomen as fear spiked.

Her baby. She'd never get to see it grow. Never have the opportunity to be a real mother to him or her. But she knew with a sudden fierce certainty that she'd do anything to protect it. Anything to ensure her baby had a good chance at life.

'Here. It's okay. We're at the car.' Thierry clicked open the lock and ushered her into the gleaming sports car that looked like something out of a glossy magazine and which she knew rode like a growling beast eager for the open road.

Suppressing a sigh of relief, she sank into the moulded leather and shut her eyes. The car dipped as he got in then he started it and swung out into the traffic.

Minutes later she opened her eyes and stared glassily at the congested traffic.

'Where are we going?'

'To your hotel. You look like you need rest, and we have to talk.'

Imogen frowned as she recognised a landmark. 'I'm not staying in the centre of the city this time.'

'Then where?'

She told him and his ebony eyebrows slashed down in a frown. 'What on earth are you doing there?'

She shrugged. 'I'd spent all my holiday money. I was due to go home, remember?' She didn't add that she'd been loath to dip into the last of her savings. She'd kept some in the bank in Australia, figuring she'd need something to cover her last months.

'Money didn't seem to be a problem before.'

Was that accusation in his voice? 'Believe it or not, I didn't stay in a five-star hotel to catch myself a rich man—'

'I didn't say that.' The wrinkle on his brow became a

scowl and it hit her that Thierry wasn't used to having his intentions questioned.

'I told you before.' She struggled for an even tone, though she felt like shouting or maybe smashing something. It was hard enough to deal with the impossible hand fate had dealt her without coping with his doubt, however reasonable. Imogen dragged in a sharp breath and tried to ignore the twin scents of luxury leather and earthy male that filled her nostrils. 'The trip was a once in a lifetime experience. I splurged on things I'd never normally afford.' She laced her fingers together in her lap. 'Now it's back to reality.'

She pursed her lips to restrain the burst of hollow laughter that threatened. If she gave in to it she feared she'd never stop but hysteria wouldn't help.

They finished the rest of the trip in silence. It continued as he unlocked the door to an apartment in a prestigious old building looking out over the Seine. One glance at the spacious living room with its view of central Paris glittering in the twilight told her she'd stepped into another world. One where wealth was figured in numbers with far more zeroes than she'd ever see.

'Please, take a seat.'

Imogen settled onto a vibrant red lounger that toned with the slash of grey, red and yellow abstract art over the fireplace. A moment later Thierry passed her a tall glass. 'Sparkling water, but I can make tea or coffee if you prefer.'

'This is fine.' Gratefully, she sipped, watching as he strode to the bar in one corner, downed a shot of something then poured himself another before turning towards her.

'Are you all right?' As soon as the words escaped, she firmed her lips. What a stupid thing to say. Of course he wasn't okay. She was still in shock and she'd had seven days to get used to her pregnancy.

Yet his eyebrows rose in surprise. Because he hadn't expected her to notice he wasn't utterly in control?

Looking at him now, at those broad shoulders that seemed capable of withstanding any weight, at the glinting dark eyes and firm jaw, she realised that, no matter how surprising her news, Thierry Girard was more than capable of handling it.

Exactly the sort of man she needed. For the first time today she felt herself begin to relax, just a little.

'You're absolutely sure it's mine?'

Imogen stiffened, her fingers gripping so hard the water in her glass threatened to slop over the side.

She met searing eyes that probed her very depths. 'For all I know there could have been a man in Venice, one in Reykjavik and one in London too.'

Imogen swallowed hard, tasting indignation. 'You think that was on my must-do list? A lover at every stop?' Despite the harshness she heard in her voice, she couldn't quite keep the wobble from it. Maybe if she was the sort of woman to fall into bed with a stranger so easily she wouldn't have expected so much from Thierry.

She gnawed her lip and dragged her gaze from his. Was she stupid, hoping he'd help? They'd had fun together but she'd been what—a diversion? An easy lay? Certainly something different from the women he was used to in his rarefied world of wealth and privilege.

With careful precision she put her glass on a nearby table and scooted to the edge of her seat, grabbing her bag from where she'd dropped it.

'Where are you going?'

Imogen blinked, sanity returning.

She didn't have the luxury of pride. This wasn't just about her. She had a baby to consider.

'Stop it.' He crossed the space between them in a couple of long strides, making her crane her neck to look up at him.

'What?' Even as she said it his thumb brushed her bottom lip, making her register the salt tang of blood in her mouth. And more, the heady taste of his skin. Imogen had to fight not to dart out her tongue for a better taste.

'Stop torturing that lovely mouth of yours.'

The unexpectedness of that made her blink and sit back. *Lovely mouth?*

'I don't…' She shook her head.

Abruptly he dropped his hand and nodded, and Imogen was horrified at her sense of loss. Surely she was stronger than this?

Her mouth trembled, and she grabbed her glass, taking a long draught of the sparkling water, telling herself the sting of it where her teeth had grazed her skin was a timely reminder that she needed focus.

She straightened her shoulders and looked at a point near his perfectly knotted tie.

'I'm happy to take a paternity test if you like.' She paused, letting that sink in. 'Then, when you believe me, I need your help.'

CHAPTER FOUR

HELP?

In the form of money, he assumed.

Thierry hadn't missed her wide-eyed appraisal of his apartment, the way her hand lingered on the plush fabric of the designer-original lounger and her eyes on the masterpiece of Modernism over the fireplace.

But, if she carried his child, why shouldn't she expect support?

He could afford it. He'd worked like the devil to turn around the family company, not just for his ageing grandparents and cousins, but for himself too. Duty had driven him, but he'd benefited. It had stunned him to discover the wealth he'd always taken for granted was in danger of slipping away while he travelled the world, following his own pursuits. Years of poor management as his grandfather's health deteriorated had taken its toll on the family fortune.

But it was safe now.

Unlike Imogen. The sudden thought disturbed him.

Pregnancy wasn't an illness. It was surely the most natural thing in the world. Yet the sight of her tension, the dark circles beneath her eyes and her pallor drew at something inside him, making him tense and restless.

He turned to stand by the windows. But it wasn't the lights of early evening that he saw. It was her wan reflection. Her shoulders hunched again and she seemed to crumple. Not at all like the vivacious Imogen he'd known.

'What sort of help do you want? To arrange an abortion?' Alone in a foreign country, she could well ask for that sort of assistance. Especially if, as she'd said, her money had run out.

Thierry knocked back a slug of cognac, surprised to discover its taste had unaccountably turned sour.

He scowled at the glass, slamming it down onto a nearby table. He still reeled from the idea of her being pregnant. He hadn't had time to begin imagining an actual child. Yet out of nowhere anger hit him. Anger that she could consider disposing of her baby. *His* baby, if his instincts were correct.

Her equanimity at the thought of a DNA test was convincing, as was his memory of her untutored loving. Imogen wasn't a woman who flitted from man to man, no matter how easily she'd fallen into his arms.

He spun around. 'Is that it? You want to get rid of the baby?'

It would solve his problems, remove any inconvenience. Yet his stomach twisted at the thought. He found himself looming over her, watching the convulsive movement of her pale throat.

'I suppose that would be a solution,' she whispered, looking down at her twisting hands. 'Maybe it's selfish to try…'

'Try what?' He hunkered before her, confused by his desire to take her in his arms even as he wanted to shake her for even considering destroying their baby.

Their baby! Was he really so easily convinced?

Perhaps he was. Adrenalin made his heart pound, just like it used to as he'd waited for the starter's signal at the beginning of a downhill race, his eyes fixed on the treacherous snowy slope before him.

He sensed, with a marrow-deep instinct he didn't even begin to fathom, that the child was his.

Imogen lifted her head and his pulse tripped. Her eyes, more green than brown, glistened over-bright and huge in her taut face.

'I'd hoped…' She shrugged. 'I want to give my baby a chance to *live*. Is that so wrong?'

'Of course not.' Her hands were cool and slight in his. He chafed them gently, telling himself relief was a natural response. 'So you want to keep the child.' He made it a statement.

'Yes. I do.' Her hands gripped his, and he was surprised at her strength. 'I want to keep it.'

'Good. That's one thing sorted.' He made his voice businesslike, as if dealing with unexpected pregnancies was no more difficult than the business challenges he handled daily.

Thierry disengaged his hands and stood. It was hard to think when Imogen clung to him, her eyes devouring him as if he were her last hope. That muddled his brain and he needed his wits.

He sank into a nearby armchair and surveyed her, wondering what it was about this woman that evoked such strong protective instincts in a man who'd spent his life avoiding any form of commitment. He'd perfected the art of being unencumbered until his *grand-père's* illness and the realisation he couldn't avoid the yoke of duty any longer.

'You want my help.'

'Yes. Please.' But instead of meeting his gaze she focused on sipping from the glass of water he'd given her. Suspicion feathered through him, an inkling she was trying to hide something.

'And what form would this assistance take?' Now would come the appeal for money. It was only natural.

She studied the glass in her hand, one finger stroking the condensation on the outside as if it fascinated her. 'I want your help if anything goes wrong.'

Thierry straightened, his hands gripping the plush arms of his chair. 'Wrong? What could go wrong?'

She shrugged, an uneven little movement. 'Things do.'

'Not often. Not with good medical care.' He frowned. Was she scared by pregnancy?

The idea confused him. Where was the woman who'd planned to skydive, climb a glacier and see volcanoes in Iceland? Who'd shown not one hint of fear as he'd taken her hot-air ballooning outside Paris?

Still she stared at the tall glass in her hands.

'Do you need money for health care? Is that it?' He'd assumed she was well-off, given where they'd met and where she'd stayed on her first visit to Paris. Now she seemed skint.

She shook her head. 'No. I should be all right once I'm back in Australia. There's comprehensive health care, plus I have some savings I haven't touched.'

Once she returned to Australia.

So, she didn't intend to stay here through her pregnancy. Thierry ignored the unfamiliar hollow sensation in his gut. It couldn't be disappointment. His lifestyle, and especially the lifestyle he was about to return to—never in one place longer than it took to conquer the next challenge—left no room for a baby. Besides, children were better off with their mothers; everyone said so. If he really wanted he could visit after it was born.

Yet discontent niggled.

And surprise. She didn't want to be with him. She didn't want his money. She only wanted his help if things went wrong.

Common sense told him he was getting out of this lightly. Most men would jump at the chance to divest themselves of such responsibilities.

But Thierry couldn't feel relief. He felt curiously deprived.

'What, exactly, do you want from me, Imogen?' At her name, she looked up, meeting his eyes squarely, and he felt a curious little thump in his chest, as if his heart had thudded too hard against his ribs.

Again that uneven little shrug. Her gaze swerved away, fixing on the view as if it fascinated her. 'I want to know you'll be there wh— if—something happens to me. I want to know you'll take care of him or her.'

She shifted in her seat, skewering him suddenly with a look he could only describe as desperate. Thierry felt the slow crawl of an icy finger up his nape, each individual hair on his neck and arms rising in response.

Not just desperation but fear. What was going on?

'I'm alone, you see. My mother and sister are dead. So if anything were to happen to me…' She swiped her bottom lip with her tongue. 'I know there are some wonderful foster parents out there, but I can't bear the thought of my baby being put into care.'

'It won't come to that. You and the child will be fine.' Thierry leaned towards her, willing her to think logically, despite the panic edging her husky voice.

He hated hearing her so desperate and fearful.

Then the full implication of her words sank in. 'You've got no one back in Australia? No family?'

'No. But I'm used to looking out for myself.' This time her jaw angled higher, as if daring him to feel sorry for her.

Thierry frowned. He might not be accustomed to taking responsibility for others—he might have spent years perfecting what *Grand-père* called his 'damned selfish bachelor lifestyle'—but the idea of Imogen, pregnant and alone, disturbed him. More than disturbed. It sent a shock wave tingling through him as if he'd touched an electric current.

'What about your father?' She'd said her mother and sister were dead but she hadn't mentioned him.

Her lips pulled taut in a grimace. 'I don't know where he is. He used to move around a lot, working in outback mines. And even if I did know how to contact him I wouldn't expect him to raise his grandchild. Not when he walked out on Mum the day he found out she was expecting twins.'

Diable! Thierry's hands closed into fists as he read the careful blankness on Imogen's face. It was the sort of blankness that hid pain, despite her matter-of-fact tone.

What sort of man deserted a woman pregnant with his children?

Then he remembered that moment of relief when he'd entertained the possibility this wasn't his baby. Or that Imogen might get rid of it and make things easier for them both. A shudder of revulsion ripped through him at the idea he had anything in common with a man like her father, even if only for a split second.

'You needn't worry about that.' His voice sounded harsh and he saw a hint of surprise on her features. 'I won't run scared.'

It was one of the things he'd always prided himself on—his ability to face fear. In his youth he'd stared it down on neck-breaking black ski-runs while the hopes of a nation weighed down his shoulders. Later there'd been adventure sports and his treks into inhospitable territory with his friend Orsino Chatsfield. More recently he'd confronted the ultimate horror: a desk job, hemmed in by solid walls while he came to grips with the ailing Girard business interests.

'You'll take care of our child if I die?'

Thierry surged to his feet. 'You're not going to die.' Years ago he'd been first on the scene in a desert car rally after a crash. The other driver had died in his arms while they'd waited for an airlift and Thierry had never felt so helpless. He refused to countenance such talk from Imogen. 'You're going to have an uneventful pregnancy, a healthy baby and a long, happy life as a mother.'

And, most probably, as someone's wife.

The realisation sent a twang of discontent through his gut.

'You sound so sure.' This time the curve of her lovely mouth, though tiny, was a real smile.

'I am.'

'Thank you, Thierry.' She looked away, but not before he saw her blink back what looked like a glimmer of moisture. Her lashes clumped as if wet, and the sight filled him with unfamiliar feelings.

'Don't.' He leaned down, taking the glass from her hand and putting it aside. Then he tugged her up till she stood before him, shorter than he remembered in her flat shoes. The scent of sweetness and vanilla filled his nostrils as he leaned close. 'There's nothing to cry about.'

Her mouth twisted in a crumpled sort of smile and her palm grazed his cheek. 'You're a good man, Thierry Girard.'

He blinked, transfixed by the mix of emotions flitting across her features. Or perhaps by the strange sensation in the pit of his stomach, as if he'd gone into freefall.

A good man? Focused, yes. Selfish, yes. With a taste for adventure and good-looking women. And an astute business sense that had surprised everyone, himself included.

Her hand began to slide away and he grabbed it, clamping it against his jaw. He liked its soft warmth against his skin.

'What's going on, Imogen?' She was hiding something. He'd read that in her refusal to hold his gaze. The way she kept looking away, as if scared he'd see too much. But what could it be? He was ready to accept the child was his, even if his lawyers would probably advise a paternity test.

'Nothing.' Her laugh sounded forced. 'Apart from an unexpected pregnancy.'

'Imogen.' He captured the back of her head in his free hand, delving his fingers into the soft luxury of her hair.

Memory hit—of those dark, silky waves slithering over them both as they'd lain naked in bed. Of him tugging gently on her hair so she arched her neck back, exposing her creamy throat to his mouth. Of the taste of her, sweet and addictive.

Fire ignited in his groin and his fingers tightened.

She could break his hold. All she had to do was step back, or tell him to let go.

The voice of reason urged him to do just that. Not to complicate an already fraught situation.

But he didn't.

He stood, looking down, watching a delicate flush steal across her cheeks, turning pallor to peaches-and-cream loveliness. And still she stood, watching him through narrowed eyes, her long dark lashes veiling her expression. She was a contradiction, a conundrum. Vulnerable yet unwavering, alluring and intriguing, a mystery to be solved.

Her lips parted, and he leaned closer, needing to taste. It had been too long.

His lips touched hers, and he realised he'd made a serious error of judgement when sensation exploded, tightening his limbs, his belly, his grip on her. His mouth moved with purpose now. Not for a whisper-soft taste, but with a ravening hunger that hadn't been assuaged since the day Imogen had left Paris.

She tasted so sweet. Lush, feminine and delicious. The scent of her intoxicated him and he bowed her back, thrusting his tongue into her mouth, shocked at how the familiar taste of her blasted at his control. A tremor passed through him, a huge, curling wave of hunger and exultation as she kissed him back, just as ravenous as he.

Her free hand slid up his chest to cup the back of his neck, fingers tight as if defying him to break away. He felt another detonation inside him, her touch, her need, triggering his to even greater heights.

Imogen made a low humming sound in the back of her throat that sent him crazy. From the first he'd lusted after her enthusiasm, her passion. He needed it now. How had he gone so long without it? She was sweet rain after drought, ambrosia after starvation.

Thierry released her hand and wrapped an arm around her, hauling her in to him so she cushioned his burgeoning arousal with her soft belly.

Her belly.

His baby.

Realisation slammed into him. Tension crawled along his limbs to grab his neck and shoulders. A new sort of tension that had nothing to do with sex.

He dragged his mouth free, hauling in air.

Hectic colour scored her cheeks and throat, and her lips were red from his kisses. Her eyelids fluttered as if reluctant to open.

He wanted to grind himself against her, strip her clothes away and lose himself in her welcoming body.

The body that cradled a fragile new life.

The body of a woman who for some reason feared this pregnancy like a physical threat.

What was he thinking?

He wasn't thinking. He was doing what he'd always done—indulging in whatever pleasure beckoned.

Abruptly, he straightened, his hands dropping, engulfed in horror at his lack of control. You'd think that in his thirties he'd have conquered the impulse to act rashly.

But one touch, one taste of Imogen, and thought fled.

He stared into dazed eyes that glowed green and honey-brown and knew he teetered on the edge of control.

Deliberately, he stepped back, his movements stiff and reluctant, forcing his brain to function. There was more he needed to understand. Much more.

'Are you going to tell me the truth now?'

'The truth?' The words sounded like a foreign language. Imogen stared at that firm mouth, the sensuous bottom lip, the taut line it formed when he stopped speaking. 'What do you mean?'

It was all she could do not to sway as she stood, bereft of his touch, still feeling his body imprinted on hers. She bit her lip, silencing the futile plea that he gather her close again.

She wanted Thierry. Wanted the comfort of him holding her, the taste of him—cognac and that bitter-chocolate tang that was unique to Thierry. She wanted to be naked with him, losing herself to ecstasy.

But he looked distant, even standing so near. His eyes were unreadable, his face taut, prouder, harder than she remembered it. Suspicious.

'What don't you want me to know? You're not telling me the truth.'

Imogen jerked back an unsteady step. Her heart thumped harder. 'I know the pregnancy is a surprise, but it's real. You heard the doctor.' Pride came to her aid, stiffening her backbone. 'Or is it the idea you're the father that you doubt?'

Had she really believed he'd take her word it was his? She pulled her arms across her chest, holding in the welling hurt.

Slowly, he shook his head, his piercing gaze never leaving her face. 'It's not that. There's something more. Something you're hiding. I won't do anything until I know what it is.'

That powerful jaw took on an obstinate cast as he crossed his arms across his chest, reinforcing that aura of tough, masculine strength despite his suavely tailored jacket. His lips thinned and his nostrils flared.

He looked intimidating. Not like the easy lover she remembered, or the passionate man of seconds ago. There was passion still, but something formidable too.

'You're reneging on what you said? You won't step in if something...happens to me?' Fear clutched. She wasn't even sure if she could carry this child to term but she had to believe she could. And she had to believe there'd be someone to care for it when she was gone.

'Hey.' His voice was soothing, his fleeting touch on her arm gentle. 'Don't get worked up. All I want is the truth. Surely I'm entitled to that?'

'You have the truth. The baby is yours.'

He stood silent, his scrutiny like a weight pushing her down.

She spun away, turning to the windows, vaguely aware of the lights of Paris beyond. Once, a few weeks ago, she'd have revelled in being here, seeing this. Now she felt terrified, scared not so much for herself as for her baby. Despair hovered in the shadows at the corner of her vision, ready to pounce if she let her guard down.

'I can't help unless you tell me what's troubling you.'

She pivoted towards him. 'Help?' She'd wondered if he was looking for an excuse to wriggle out of that.

'I said I would and I'm a man of my word.' He spoke with such authority she couldn't help but believe him.

Imogen hadn't wanted to tell him too soon, scared the knowledge he'd definitely be responsible for their child might frighten him off. Yet surely he deserved to know? The sooner he came to grips with what was to come, the better.

'Whatever it is, I'm sure it'll be okay.'

A laugh ripped from Imogen's throat. The sound scared her—so raw and guttural. It betrayed the fact she clung to calm by the skin of her teeth.

Thierry's dark eyebrows shot up, his gaze interrogative.

'It won't be okay, that's the problem.' Her voice was harsh and raspy. She cleared her throat. 'I'm not going to be a mother and I'm not going to know my child.' Pain settled like a lump of cold metal in her stomach, its chill paralysing. 'I'm dying.'

CHAPTER FIVE

THE NEXT HOUR passed in a haze, for which Imogen was grateful. She'd had enough of pain and grief and though both still threatened like bullies hovering at the edge of a playground, Thierry's presence kept them at bay.

Two things stood out. First, the way he'd gone stark white beneath the bronze of his tanned olive skin when he heard her news. Even the laughter lines at the corners of his eyes had morphed into creases that betrayed shock rather than humour. Second, his gentle solicitude as he'd ushered her back to a chair and pressed a hot drink into her hands.

His touch had been impersonal, as far from his earlier passionate grip as it was possible to be. Dying did that—it distanced you from people, putting up an unseen but unbreakable barrier no one wanted to broach. She'd seen it with her mother—people keeping their distance, as if they feared her brain tumour might be catching.

In Thierry's case, the fire died out of his eyes as she told him about her condition, and that her mother had died of the same illness just months before. He hadn't protested in disbelief but his face had grown grimmer and grimmer as she'd spelled out what was in store.

'We need to get you to a specialist.' Even his voice had changed, the timbre hollow instead of smooth and rich.

She leaned her head against the back of her chair. 'I have another appointment in Sydney in a couple of weeks.'

'So far away?'

She shrugged. 'I'm not in a hurry, Thierry. I've been through it all with my mother and I know what to expect. Except...' She pressed a hand to her stomach, terror swooping through her as she thought of the danger to her baby.

'Don't.' He hunkered beside her, his hand on hers firm and strong, callused, as if he did more with his time than attend meetings. Heat seeped from his touch. She imagined it as warm tendrils shooting and unfurling, spreading through her chilled body. Was it imagination or did the tightness around her hunched shoulders ease?

Then he said something that threatened to undo her.

'You're not alone now, Imogen.'

He made no ridiculous promises to find a cure when there was none, to snatch her from the jaws of death. That would have meant nothing, just the bluster of someone unwilling to accept the inevitable.

Instead, his words pierced the shaky wall she'd built around her heart. They made her feel less desperate.

She opened her mouth to tell him how precious a gift he'd given her but found she couldn't speak. She gulped down a knot of emotion.

She'd known this man a few short weeks and yet for the first time since she'd lost her mother—in fact since Isabelle had died—she felt something like whole.

'You need to rest. You're exhausted.'

It was true. Sleep had eluded her this week. As if on cue, a mighty yawn rose.

'You're right. I'd better get back to the hotel.'

For answer Thierry slid his arms beneath her and hoisted her up in one smooth movement as he stood. His darkening jaw was just centimetres away and beneath the hand she pressed to his chest came the steady thud of his heartbeat.

Safe, it seemed to say.

For once Imogen let herself ignore the tiny voice of reality that sneered nothing could keep her safe now. Instead, she let her head sink against his shoulder. Just for a moment it was nice to be cared for. It was a novelty she could get used to.

Except she wouldn't have the chance to get used to it, would she?

He must have heard her hiccup of laughter.

'What is it?'

'Nothing. I'm just tired.'

'Which is why you're going to bed.' He turned and carried her from the room. To her amazement they didn't head towards the foyer but down a wide corridor.

'Thierry? I need to get back to my hotel.'

He stopped. 'Why? Have you got medicine there that you need?'

She shook her head.

'Good. You can sleep here. I'll lend you something to wear and bring you supper once you're in bed.'

Imogen knew she should move, knew she couldn't afford to get used to being cosseted. It would only make things more difficult later. But what woman would willingly give up the pleasure of being in Thierry's powerful arms, even for a short time?

The beautiful bedroom with its high ceilings, elegant doors and honey-coloured wood flooring spoke of the elegance of another age, even if the *en suite* bathroom she glimpsed was all modern luxury. One quick survey told her this was a guest room. No sign of Thierry's personal belongings. Nor could she imagine him choosing the delicate pale blue and cream bed linens for himself.

He lowered her onto a bed that her weary bones protested was just too comfortable to leave.

Would it be so wrong to stay the night? Independence warred with exhaustion as she sat, swaying.

'Here. You can use this tonight.' She hadn't even noticed Thierry leave but he was entering the room again. He pressed something soft into her hands, and she looked down, seeing a black T-shirt that she knew would look fantastic clinging to his hard chest. Her pulse did the funny little jig that had become familiar during her time in Paris. *He* did that to her.

She looked up into burning dark eyes. Concern etched

his face. She wanted to assure him everything would be okay, erase the pain that turned his mouth into a sombre line, but she couldn't find any words to make this right.

Instead, she conjured a half-smile. 'Thank you, Thierry.' She paused, letting herself enjoy the sound of his name on her tongue. Soon she'd have no reason to use it, once she was back home. She shifted, forcing her heavy eyelids up, squaring her shoulders. 'It's thoughtful of you. I'd very much like to stay the night.'

Her hands tightened on the T-shirt. So what if a night of being cared for made the solitude she faced later harder to bear? She'd rather experience these past couple of hours with him, even if only in his apartment, not sharing his bed, than the emptiness of that soulless hotel room.

But it was more than a couple of hours. When the sun rose so did Imogen, staggering a little, groping along the wall as she made her way to the bathroom.

The headache was back. Amazingly, it was the first in weeks, but it clawed at her skull as if some giant bird of prey dug hot talons into her brain.

She was back in bed when the bedroom door opened. Thierry's hair was damp and gleaming black. Tailored charcoal trousers clung to solid thighs and his crisp white shirt revealed a V of tanned flesh where the buttons hadn't all been done up. Despite the miasma of pain, Imogen felt a twinge of pleasure at the sight of him. She regretted now that she had no photo of him. Taking holiday snaps to pore over later hadn't occurred to her. She'd spent her time trying not to think about the future.

'How are you doing?' He sat on the bed and even through the light blanket she felt his warmth. She wanted to snuggle into him and hold him tight, never let go.

She snared a breath. She had to be stronger than that. She couldn't rely on him or anyone else.

Imogen looked up through slitted eyes and read worry on his broad brow.

'Fine,' she lied, loath to make that worry worse. 'Just tired.' That, at least, was true. A week of little sleep had left her on the edge of exhaustion.

A hand brushed the hair from her face, and her eyes fluttered closed. His touch was so soothing, so gentle. Yearning rose in a welling tide.

'Are you sure that's all? Do you need a doctor?'

Her eyes sprang open to find him leaning closer, the spicy fresh scent of his skin making her nostrils flare.

'No doctor. I've had enough of them for now.' Sydney would be soon enough. 'I'm fine, really, just tired.'

'I've brought croissants and juice if you're hungry.' She shook her head, and he frowned. 'I have appointments all morning. I could put them off.'

'Don't be silly.' She tried to sound firm and strong but she suspected her voice was too hoarse. 'I'll get up now and head back to my hotel.'

'You really think I'd let you?'

'Sorry?' Was the ache in her head making her hear things?

'What sort of man do you take me for?' Anger sparked in that gleaming gaze. 'You'll stay here while you're in Paris. I'm just trying to work out whether I can leave you this morning.'

'Of course you can leave me. I'm not your responsibility.' Her brain told her to move, not loll here basking in his concern. But her aching head and tired body didn't want to move. She forced herself to pluck at the blanket, lifting it, ready to get up.

A hard hand clasped her wrist, forcing it and the blanket back down.

'Don't.' His voice caressed rather than ordered, and to her shock, awareness, acute and devastating, jagged through her. 'We'll argue about it later, when you have more energy.' He stroked her hair again and there was magic in his touch. She felt the tension rolling away in little waves. 'For now you need sleep. Promise me you'll stay here till I come back.'

It was pure weakness, she knew, but Imogen was barely surprised to hear the whisper emerge from her lips. 'Just for a while, then.'

When she finally woke, late in a golden afternoon, she was surprised to find herself refreshed, without that horrible hangover feeling after too much pain. Thankful for small mercies, she headed to the bathroom, only to discover her toiletries bag sitting there, and her hair brush. Dazed, she swivelled, looking back through the door to the bedroom. Her suitcase lay, unzipped, on the other side of the room.

He'd gone to her hotel and collected her belongings?

How had he done it? Surely there were rules about not giving strangers access to other people's hotel rooms?

Imogen's brow pleated as she tried to work out how Thierry had done it. And why. It was high-handed, and she should be annoyed, but right now the thought of getting into fresh clothes was just too appealing.

Shaking her head, she stripped off, stepping into the marble-lined shower and a stream of blissfully warm water. She'd work it all out when she was fully awake. But she'd bet Thierry's ability to access her things had something to do with that combination of innate authority and his bone-melting smile. No doubt the hotel employee he'd approached was female.

The thought stirred unwelcome feelings. A jab of what felt like jealousy.

Imogen caught herself up sharply. She had no right to jealousy. Thierry had never been hers in any real sense. Anyway, she wouldn't be with him long enough to worry about other women.

Emerging from the bathroom, she automatically reached

for jeans, then paused as she noticed the gorgeous light of late afternoon slanting in the big windows.

She'd been too exhausted yesterday to worry about anything but confronting Thierry and breaking her news. Now she needed to book a flight to Sydney since she had Thierry's word he'd care for their baby.

Which meant this could be her last evening in Paris.

Firming her lips, she put the jeans down and delved into the big suitcase. If this was her last night here…

Fifteen minutes later she stared at herself in the mirror. Izzy's dress in uncrushable scarlet lace clung more than Imogen had anticipated. And it was more suited to evening than late afternoon.

But she didn't care. Red would give her energy and the bravado she needed. Besides, she'd always loved the colour, even though back home she would never consider it. It was so attention-grabbing. So not her.

She loved it. Her last night in Paris; she refused to spend it looking like some quaking little mouse.

Thierry looked up at the sound of footsteps. Not merely footsteps but the tap of high heels, if he was any judge, which he was. His lovers all wore heels. Except Imogen, he realised. She'd been just as likely to turn up wearing flats or tennis shoes, because she was as interested in hot-air ballooning and picnicking as she was in dancing and dining.

No tennis shoes now. His heart revved to a thundering roar as a vision in red appeared in the doorway. Voluptuous, glorious, sexy as hell. The colour was a perfect contrast to the creamy swell of her breasts above the low, square-cut neckline.

She'd left her hair down. It rippled in ebony silk waves around her shoulders.

Thierry's groin tightened. Imogen only wore her hair loose in bed. That had been his secret pleasure, inhaling its indefinable sweet fragrance, rubbing it between his fingers, feeling its caress on his bare skin as they made love.

His gaze dropped to the hemline above her knees and her long, shapely legs. To scarlet stilettos.

His breath rushed out like air from a punctured balloon. Arousal vied with disbelief.

How could she look this way when she was *dying*? The word hung like a dark stain on his consciousness, tearing at his innards, making his gut writhe in denial.

All night and day he'd fought to come to grips with her news. Even now part of him rejected the prognosis as impossible. *Not Imogen.*

'You look stunning.' The words jerked out hoarsely.

She stopped, eyes rounding. 'I do?' Something that might have been pleasure flitted across her face. 'Thank you. I needed something to give me courage for my last night in Paris. I wanted to look…' she shrugged '…well.'

Instantly, guilt rose. Because he was busy lusting after a fatally ill woman. Because he couldn't get up from the seat where he was working on a report for fear she'd see just how well he thought she looked. He scrubbed a hand across his jaw, trying to reorient himself.

'You look more than well. You look blooming.' The red brought colour to her cheeks and the long sleep had lessened the shadows beneath her fine eyes. Savagely he squashed the temptation to stride across and haul her to him, to claim those lips he knew would be soft and inviting, to explore that glorious body.

Because she was dying. The word scourged his brain.

'Sorry? I missed that.' He knew she'd spoken but the rush of blood in his ears had deafened him.

'I asked if you have wi-fi. I need to book my flight home.' She lifted one hand and rubbed her bare arm, as if to counteract a chill. 'I *should* argue about the fact you collected my luggage without permission. And I should move back to the hotel.' She paused, turning towards the window. 'But I don't want to waste time. This will probably be my last night in France and I've got other things to do.'

'Other things?' Dressed like that? He shot to his feet, his papers sliding to the floor. 'Like what?' The way she looked, she'd have men clustered around her the moment she stepped out the door.

A tiny, self-conscious smile lit her face, and Thierry felt as if someone had reached in and grabbed his innards. How much longer would she be able to smile like that?

'I was so busy when I was here last time, I never took one of those dinner cruises on the Seine, even though it was on my list of things to do.'

Was that a hint of a blush? Was she too thinking of all the things they'd done instead of cruising the river?

It was on the tip of Thierry's tongue to say those cruises were crowded with tourists, and the loudspeaker commentary would detract from the ambience of the evening, but he firmed his lips. He wasn't going to spoil it for her.

'So, wi-fi?' She moved farther into the room and Thierry had to force his gaze up to her face instead of on the undulating curves outlined in the tight red dress.

He dragged open his collar as heat rose. She looked so sultry and alluring it was hard to believe she carried a new life inside. Or that she was gravely ill.

Even his lawyer's dire warnings about paternity tests wouldn't stop him doing what he could for her. He'd been told he had no duty to her legally. But legalities weren't the issue.

'I can do better than that.' He cleared his throat, conscious his voice sounded gruff. 'I'll have my PA make the arrangements if you bring me your passport. She can book a dinner cruise too.'

'She's still working?' Imogen glanced at her watch.

'I usually keep much longer business hours than this.' He'd cut them back when she'd been in Paris last time, working like a demon all day so he could have his evenings free for her. He stooped to pick up the reports he'd dropped and put them on the table. 'Mademoiselle Janvier will still be at work, believe me.'

'As long as I can pay you for the air fare.'

Thierry looked at her, standing proud in her high heels. This woman admitted she needed courage to face her last night in Paris and that she was short of cash, yet she refused to take charity when it would be so easy and reasonable.

His heart dipped and skidded to a halt, only to start up again in an uneven rhythm.

She was a wonder. He'd never known a woman like her. Except perhaps his *grand-mère*, whose petite size and exquisite manners hid a spine of steel.

Would he exhibit such courage in Imogen's situation? It was one thing to risk his neck in some dangerous adventure, quite another to be stoic in the face of a steady, fatal decline. The thought of what she faced curdled his blood.

'I'll make sure you get the bill for any air fare.' As if that was going to happen. 'Now, if you'll get me your passport, I'll contact my PA.'

'I don't know which is better, the *tarte tatin* or the scenery.' Imogen sat back, replete, looking from her empty plate to the beautiful, floodlit bridge they were about to pass under. A series of pale, carved stone heads stared sightlessly out from its side, intriguing her. 'I knew the Eiffel Tower looked terrific lit up, and Notre Dame and all the other buildings, but these bridges are amazing.'

Silently she vowed to store the memory of this last night with Thierry to pull out and remember later, when her condition worsened and the shadows closed in.

'So…' Beside her Thierry lifted his glass and sipped. 'It's not the company you're enjoying?'

When he looked at her that way, his eyes gleaming and that hint of a cleft grooving his cheek as he smiled, Imogen's heart leapt. In the subtle light of the lanterns on deck he looked suavely sophisticated. Yet Imogen knew from experience that his rangy frame, which showed off a dinner jacket to perfection, was actually a symphony of lean, hard-packed muscle and bone. He might look indolent but the man beneath the sophisticated exterior had the body of an athlete, and such strength…

Desperately, she dragged her eyes away. Pregnancy, like illness, had no effect on her attraction to him. If anything her response was sharper, more urgent. Because she'd developed a craving for his love-making and, just as importantly, because he made her feel *special.*

'Are you after a compliment?' Imogen forced herself to smile, hiding her tumble of emotions. Desire, gratitude, piercing regret and that undercurrent of fear. Once she left him she'd face her future alone. She squared her shoulders. 'It's wonderful of you to make my last night in Paris so memorable. I can't tell you how much it means.'

'You already have.' A casual gesture dismissed what he'd done as negligible. But Imogen was no fool. She'd been about to use the last of her available money to pay for a package tourist-trip. Instead, she'd found herself on a private luxury cruiser where they were the only guests, waited on by superb staff and eating one of the best meals of her life. The cost must have been exorbitant.

She leaned forward, reaching for Thierry's arm, till she realised what she was doing and grabbed her water glass instead.

'Don't brush it off as nothing, Thierry. What you've done…' To her horror she felt her throat thicken. 'You should at least let me thank you.'

Over the rim of his glass, Thierry's eyes locked with hers and a tingle of sensation shot through her, spreading to her breasts before arrowing to her womb. Imogen sucked in a stunned breath. Her body's urgent response to him threatened to unravel her totally.

Even the knowledge her condition had apparently killed

his desire for her couldn't stop that throb of feminine wanting. She'd read his closed expression and understood he saw her as a victim, a figure of pity, not a desirable woman.

'You want to thank me?' He put his glass down and leaned close. Too close, but she couldn't seem to pull back. 'Good. Because there's something I want you to do.'

'There is?' She couldn't imagine what. Unless, of course, it was the DNA test to prove paternity. She'd heard there were risks involved with those during pregnancy but if it meant giving her child a secure future…

'Yes.' He paused so long tension tightened the bare skin of her shoulders. 'I want you to marry me.'

There was a thud and cold liquid spilled onto her thigh. Vaguely Imogen was aware of Thierry reaching out to grab her water glass before it could roll onto the deck.

She didn't move, just sat, goggling.

'Ah, thank you.' He spoke to the waiter who appeared out of nowhere to mop the tablecloth and clear the plates. All the while Thierry sat there, leaning back now, one arm looped casually over the back of his chair, watching her.

The waiter left.

'What did you say?' Her voice was a croak from constricted muscles.

'I want us to marry. This week.'

He looked so relaxed, as if he'd merely commented on the quality of the meal they'd shared, or on the beautiful old buildings floodlit along the banks of the Seine.

Her pulse fluttered like a mad thing. 'You can't be serious.'

'Never more so.' They approached another bridge and for a few moments were bathed in light. That was when she saw it, the glint of determination in those espresso-dark eyes. And the arrogant thrust of his chin.

Imogen wasn't aware of moving but she heard a scrape and suddenly she was on her feet, stumbling for the deck's rail. She clutched it with hands that shook.

She didn't know what she felt. This was one shock too many. Her legs wobbled and she had trouble dragging in enough oxygen.

'There's no need for that,' she finally gasped out. 'Is this you trying to be kind?' She didn't need pity, no matter how good his intentions.

Imogen spun around, only to find Thierry standing behind her, just a breath away. His clean scent filled her senses as she fought for air.

'Not kind. Just practical. Planning for the future.' His voice was smoothly persuasive. Dully, she wondered if he used this tone to broker his business deals. Yet, despite his calm demeanour, she sensed he wasn't as relaxed as he appeared.

Good! *Her* heart was racing like a runaway train.

Imogen shook her head. 'I don't see what's practical about it.' She licked dry lips, peering up into his shadowed features. 'When the time comes… I'll ensure you're named as the father and—'

'You think it will be that easy? Claiming the child from the other side of the world? No matter what the birth certificate says, I'll bet Australian law is every bit as complex as in France. There'll be one hurdle after another for me to claim the baby. It could take months, years.'

The baby. Not *his* baby.

What had she expected? That a mere twenty-four hours after learning he was going to be a father, Thierry would have the same powerful connection she felt for the tiny life inside her? Of course it was too much to ask. All she could do was hope that with time that would change.

'Do you want to risk the possibility your baby will be put in care while the legalities are sorted out?'

Pain scoured her, as if someone took a rusty blade and scraped it through her womb. Her palm found her belly, pressing tenderly as if to make sure that little life was safe inside.

A large hand, warm and callused, covered hers, splaying gently across her abdomen. She blinked and looked up into unreadable eyes.

'If we marry there will be no legal hurdles. I'll be responsible for our child. There will be no waiting, no complications. Only what's best for the baby.' Thierry's voice dropped to a low, crooning note that flowed through her like molten chocolate. Or maybe that was the effect of his touch, so real, so *sure*.

'You know there's a chance the baby might not survive?' She choked back the horror that had haunted her since she'd learned of her pregnancy. The fear that her child might die simply because she wouldn't live long enough for it to survive.

In the gloom away from the lights, she could just make out the fierce jut of Thierry's hard jaw.

When he spoke his voice held an edge she couldn't identify. 'As your husband, I'll be in a position to do everything possible for it. And for you.'

For one enticing moment Imogen let herself imagine leaning on Thierry as she had today, allowing him to take care of her. But ultimately they were strangers.

'I don't belong here, Thierry. My home is in Australia.'

'Yet you admit you've got no one to look after you there.'

'You think I came to Paris to find someone who'd look after me?' She tried to free her hand from his but he simply pressed closer, crowding her against the railing. 'I'm Australian. I belong there.'

'And who will care for you?' His words were like soft blows, hammering at her. 'You have no family. Have you close friends who'll be there whenever you need them? Have you got *anyone*?'

Said like that, he made her sound so pathetic. 'My really good friends have all moved away with jobs or family.' And, while she got on well with her work colleagues, this last year she'd been so wrapped up in grief after Izzy's death, then busy caring for her mother, that she'd got out of the habit of accepting social invitations. She'd effectively cut herself off. 'But I'll be fine. The health service—'

'I'm not talking about people paid to look after you.' His fingers closed around hers and he lifted her hand between them. To her surprise he planted her palm against his mouth and pressed a kiss to it. A kiss that sent heat and wonder coursing through her, reminding her she wasn't dead yet.

'I'm talking about someone who will be there for you. Someone who can deal with the medicos when you're too weary. Someone who'll be on hand to look after our child.'

Imogen's heart swelled. Put that way, the offer was irresistible.

'You know I'm right, Imogen.' His lips moved against her sensitive palm and the low burr of his voice curled around her like an embrace. And something inside, some selfish, needy part of her, urged her to accept.

Silently, she nodded.

An instant later his arms closed about her, pulling her against his hard chest.

Relief filled her. She just hoped she wasn't making a mistake they'd both regret.

CHAPTER SIX

BY SATURDAY THEY were married.

Thierry steered his car through the congestion of central Paris, hyperaware of the woman beside him, her belongings stored neatly in the back.

He was a married man.

Married and expecting a child.

His hands clamped the wheel. Sweat beaded his hairline and something like panic stirred. Him—responsible for raising a child? The notion was so far out of left field, he still couldn't quite believe it. He could face any number of extreme sports with a thrill of anticipation, yet the idea of being solely responsible for another life filled him with trepidation. He had no experience with kids, no desire for…

He caught the direction of his thoughts and cut it off. Shame pierced him, curdling his belly. So what if he knew nothing about child-rearing? He'd adapt. He'd take it one step at a time, just as he had when forced by injury to give up competitive skiing, and when he'd taken charge of the ailing family company. He had no right to complain, not when Imogen…

No, he refused to go there, at least today. For now it was enough that she was here with him. He was doing what needed to be done, despite his legal advisor's warnings.

He'd never had much time for lawyers. But to be fair the old man had probably been as stunned by his news as Thierry's family would be.

Thierry was the bachelor least likely to tie the knot, much to his grandparents' despair. In his youth he'd vowed never to settle for any other woman since he couldn't have Sandrine. Looking back on that time now, he felt merely curiosity and a twinge of remembered disappointment at the hurt which he'd thought had blighted his life.

How naïve he'd been. Far from being destroyed, his life had been filled to the brim. He'd spent the intervening years doing exactly what he loved—feeding his appetite for pleasure: sport, women, adventure.

'You look happy.'

He turned to see Imogen scrutinising him, as if trying to read him. Why wouldn't she? She'd put her life in his hands, and their child's life.

She'd put on a good show of being indomitable these past few days, but her tiredness betrayed her. He couldn't bear to think of where that would inevitably lead. The knowledge had been like acid eating at him ever since he'd heard. He'd never felt so appallingly *useless*.

'Getting out of the city is cause for celebration, don't you think?' He forced a smile and was rewarded with a slight upward tilt of her lips.

He'd always liked the way she responded to his smile, even when, as now, he guessed she felt out of sorts.

Out of sorts! His smile twisted.

'You don't like the city? I think Paris is fabulous.'

Thierry shrugged, focusing his attention on the road and the van trying to change lanes into a non-existent space between a motorcycle and another car.

'To visit, perhaps, but where we're going there'll be pure air. No fumes or road noise. No crowds either.'

'I thought you enjoyed socialising.'

He shrugged, taking action to avoid a kamikaze motorcyclist. 'I love a good party, but after a while I've had enough of the chatter.'

'So what do you like, then?'

A sideways glance showed her turned towards him, her gaze curious, as if she really wanted to know.

It struck him that most of the women he'd known had had their own agendas—to be seen at the right parties or with the right people, the heir to the Girard fortune being one of the right people. They'd had fun together but how many had tried to know Thierry the man rather than Thierry the CEO or Thierry the scion of one of France's elite families? Or, in the old days, Thierry the famous athlete?

'Surely it's not a hard question?'

Not hard at all. 'Skiing. Downhill and very, very fast.' Once he'd thought that was his destiny. He'd been in the peak of his form training for the Winter Olympics before a busted leg had put an end to those dreams.

'What else?'

Another glance showed she hadn't taken her eyes off him. Of course she wanted to know. He'd be the one raising their child. His hands tightened on the wheel.

'White-water rafting. Rally driving. Rock climbing.'

'You don't like to be still.'

'You could say that. Except for hot-air ballooning. There's nothing quite like that for getting a little perspective in your life.' He didn't add that a lot of his balloon treks took him to inhospitable, often dangerous places where tourists rarely went.

'And when you're not outdoors?'

'These days I'm usually working.' In the past he'd have unwound in the company of some gorgeous woman but lately his interest had waned. Until Imogen. Even today, in jeans and a plain shirt, her lithe curves made his hands itch for physical contact.

Not even telling himself that it was wrong to lust after a dying woman, a woman relying on him, could kill that hot flare of hunger.

'What about you, Imogen? What do you like to do? I don't mean the things on your travel list.' It struck him suddenly that hers really had been a bucket list to be accomplished before she died. The realisation was like an icy hand curling gnarled fingers around his chest, squeezing till his lungs burned.

'You mean, in my ordinary life?'

Thierry nodded, not trusting his voice.

'The list is pretty ordinary, like me. No white-water rafting.'

'*Ordinary* isn't the way I'd describe you, Imogen.' Not with her zest for life, her sense of humour and that entrancing mix of pragmatism and wide-eyed enthusiasm. As for her body… He couldn't go there, not if he wanted to keep his wits on the traffic.

She laughed, but the smoky quality of her voice held a harsh rasp. 'I suppose you think I'm more like a walking disaster zone. Suddenly you've been saddled with—'

'Don't!' Thierry dragged in a breath that grated across his throat. This wasn't the place to rehash their debate about her being a burden. He knew this was the right thing and he refused to resile from that. He forced a smile into his voice. 'You don't get out of answering that easily. Tell me at least three things that make you happy.'

In his peripheral vision, he saw Imogen slump a little in her seat. Then she turned to stare out the window.

'Books. I love reading, anything from romance to history or biography.'

'And? That's only one.'

She hesitated. 'Numbers. I've always liked numbers. There's something…comfortable about working with figures and finding the patterns that create order out of chaos. I suppose that's why I went into accounting.'

Thierry nodded. His cousin, Henri, was the same. Give him a spreadsheet and he was happy. The trouble was, though Henri was a genius with figures, he showed little aptitude for management. Lately it had become obvious that Thierry's plan of leaving the family company in his charge was fraught with problems.

'And the third?'

'Baking. Well, cooking generally, but baking specifically.'

'What do you bake?' Thierry was intrigued. He didn't know anyone who cooked for pleasure.

He thought of Jeanne, who'd been his grandparents' cook as long as he could remember. She was fiercely protective of her domain, a dumpy little woman with arms as strong as any farm labourer, and fingers that could pinch a boy's ears painfully if he wasn't quick enough stealing fresh-baked pastries. As far as he could tell, she had nothing in common with Imogen.

'Anything. Kneading bread dough is therapeutic but I love making sweet things, like baklava or Danishes. I always get requests at work for my honey-chocolate sponge cake.'

How apt that she tasted like one of her pastries—of vanilla and sugar. Except Imogen was more delectable than any cake he'd ever eaten.

It had been days since he'd tasted her. Yet, despite his determination not to press her when she was unwell, Thierry's craving for her sweet lips had grown, not eased, with abstinence.

'So, I'm pretty boring, really.'

He flicked on the car's indicator and changed lanes, accelerating as they left the city behind.

'You're anything but boring.' Thierry paused, mulling over what she'd told him. 'You like being at home.'

'I suppose so.'

'Tell me about it. What's your home like?'

Imogen shifted in her seat. 'I was saving up for a place of my own when this… When I decided to come to France. I'd been renting, sharing a flat, but I moved back in with my mother while she was ill.'

In other words she'd nursed her mother through her decline. What must it be like, after watching her mother's fatal deterioration, to know in intimate detail what she herself could expect?

Thierry put his foot to the floor and for a short time focused on the satisfying distraction of speed. But it didn't work. His thoughts kept circling back to Imogen.

'Your family home, then. What was it like?'

Again that short laugh, a little ragged around the edges. 'We didn't have one. We moved too often.'

He shot her a questioning look.

'My mother worked hard to qualify as a teacher when Isabelle and I were little, but she had trouble getting a permanent position. She never said so but it might have been because of the demands of raising twins. Anyway, she worked as a casual teacher, filling in where needed, sometimes for a term at a time if we were lucky.'

'In Sydney?'

'All around the state, though in later years she worked in Sydney. By then she'd come to enjoy the challenge of dealing with new pupils and new surroundings all the time. She chose to keep working on short-term placements.'

'Maybe that explains the bond between you all.'

'Sorry?'

'When you speak of your mother or sister I hear affection in your voice. I get the impression you were close.'

She was silent for a few moments. 'I suppose it did draw us closer together in some ways.'

'But not all?' Thierry passed a slow-moving truck then rolled his shoulders. Already he felt a familiar sense of release at leaving Paris.

'Isabelle thrived on new places, making new friends, starting afresh. She was the outgoing one.'

'You're not outgoing?' He thought of her laughter the night they'd met in Paris, the confident way she'd bantered with him. Plus there was the enthusiastic way she embraced every new experience.

Out of the corner of his eye he saw her rub her palm

down her jeans. He jerked his attention back to the road, before his mind wandered to places it shouldn't.

'I'm the reserved one, the cautious twin. Izzy would walk into a new classroom and by the end of the day she'd have five new best friends. It would take me weeks or months, and by that stage we'd usually be on the move again. My sister thought it a grand adventure but I…suppose I just wanted more stability and certainty.'

Hence the affinity for creating order out of chaos with numbers. Thierry tried to imagine what it must have been like for such a child, averse to change, being carted around the countryside. It didn't escape him that her other interests—reading and baking—were home-based. It was a wonder she'd crossed the globe in search of adventure.

As if she'd read his thoughts, she spoke. 'My sister followed her dream and took the gamble of coming to France, hoping to work in fashion, though everyone said her chances were slim. I was the one who stayed where I was.'

'I was always looking for adventure,' he said then paused, surprised he'd shared that.

'What sort of adventure?'

'Anything to break the monotony of home.' He sensed her surprise and shot her an amused glance. 'My childhood was the opposite of yours. Everything in my world was so stable it was almost petrified. Things were done the same way they'd always been done.'

If it had been good enough for the Girards to dine in the blue salon a hundred and fifty years ago, the Girards would continue to do so, even if it was a cold room that missed the evening sun in summer. Male Girards entered the diplomatic corps or the military before taking their place managing one of the family enterprises and there was an end to it. Rules covered everything, from his choice of friends to his behaviour in public and in private.

His parents had died when he was a baby so he'd been brought up by his strict grandparents. A psychologist might say he'd rebelled against their outmoded rules and restrictions. But Thierry was pretty sure he'd simply been born with a thirst for adventure.

'We weren't big on family traditions.' Imogen's voice was soft. 'Except spending Christmas Day together, and Easter. Even in the last couple of years the three of us would have an Easter egg hunt in the garden.'

'Your mother too?'

'Of course. She loved chocolate.'

Thierry tried and failed to imagine his *grand-mère* hunting for eggs in their exquisitely kept grounds.

'That sounds like fun. I've never been on an Easter egg hunt.'

'You haven't?' Her face swung towards him again. 'It's not a French tradition?'

'For some. But not in the Girard family.' Easter had meant his best behaviour and, of course, formal clothes. He couldn't recall a time when he hadn't been expected to wear a tie to dinner. No wonder yanking his top button undone was always the first thing he did on leaving the office.

He saw her hand swipe the leg of her jeans again. 'You make your family sound a little daunting.' She paused. 'Are they?' Was that concern in her voice?

Daunting? He supposed his grandparents were, with their formality and strict adherence to old ways, but for all that he loved them.

'They'll welcome you with open arms. They've all but given up on the idea of me bringing home a bride. But you needn't worry for now. My grandparents spend the summer at their villa on the south coast. And my cousins, aunts and uncles live elsewhere.'

'You share a house with your grandparents?' Surprise tinged her tone. Who could blame her? Until four years ago he'd lived his own life, visiting the Girard estate only occasionally. But it was easier to manage the estate and the family's diverse commercial interests from there since that was where the main offices were located.

'You think it unusual for a thirty-four-year-old?' His smile was tight as he remembered how reluctant that move back home had been. 'My grandfather had a stroke a few years ago and they needed me. But don't worry; we'll be quite private. There's plenty of space.' Even when his grandparents were in residence the place was so big he could go for weeks without seeing them.

Thierry considered explaining to Imogen just what to expect. But she'd been pale today, admitting to a little nausea, which to his astonishment had evoked a visceral pang of possessiveness in him. As if it made the idea of their child suddenly more concrete. She'd been nervous too. Better not to overload her with details. He couldn't guess whether she'd be excited or retreat mentally, as she'd done a few times when unsure of herself.

'Why don't you close your eyes and rest? We'll be travelling for a while.'

The sun still shone brightly when Imogen woke. Her head lolled against the backrest. She hadn't slept well lately but the rhythm of the car had lulled her into relaxation.

She blinked. The rhythm had changed, as if the road surface was different. When she looked through the windscreen she realised they'd left the main *autoroute*. They were in what looked like a park. Great swathes of grass with tall, mature trees dotted the scene. They clustered close to the road.

She frowned. Though paved, it was a narrow road with no lines marked.

'Are we almost there?'

'Almost. You'll see it soon.'

It? Imogen felt befuddled, shreds of sleep still clinging. Presumably he meant the town where he…

She gasped as the car topped a rise and the vista opened up. Her eyes popped.

'You live in a castle?' It couldn't be...but the road they were on—a private road, she realised belatedly—headed straight for the next rise where the sun shone off massive walls of darkest honey gold.

She swung around to Thierry but he looked unmoved, as if driving home to a medieval fortification was an everyday occurrence.

She sat back in her seat, her brain buzzing.

'I don't suppose your place is off to the side somewhere? An estate manager's house or something?'

His mouth quirked up in a smile, and he slanted an amused look at her. She felt its impact deep inside as her internal organs began to liquefy.

He only has to smile and you lose it.

No wonder you let him convince you to go along with this absurd idea.

Even now, hours after the short civil ceremony, she had trouble believing she'd actually married Thierry.

'Are you disappointed? Would you rather live in a cottage?'

Slowly, she shook her head, drinking in his profile as he turned back to the road. A castle. Maybe that explained that air of assurance she'd noticed in him from the first. It was more than just the insouciance that came from looking staggeringly handsome in bespoke formal wear, or the comfortable-in-his-skin athleticism of his magnificent body. It was something bred in the bone. And then there were his strongly sculpted features. Were they the result of generations of aristocratic breeding?

'Imogen? You don't like it?'

She turned her head. The walls rose several stories and were punctuated, not with tiny arrow slits, but with large windows that must let in a lot of light. Yet at the corners of the building were sturdy round towers topped with conical roofs, like an illustration of Rapunzel's story.

'I don't know. I can't imagine actually living in a castle.'

'We call it a *château*.'

'Okay, then. I can't imagine living in a *château*.' Imogen half expected to wake up and find she'd dreamt it. A *château*! The word conjured images of royal courts and lavish indulgence. Could anything be more different from the two-bedroom flat she'd shared in suburban Sydney?

'It's like living anywhere else except it costs a lot more to heat and the maintenance bills are a nightmare. But don't worry.' Imogen heard the current of amusement in Thierry's voice. 'It's been modernised through the years. It's even got hot- and cold-running water.'

'I wouldn't expect anything less.' She recalled Thierry's Paris apartment where her bathroom had been expensively modern bordering on sybaritic decadence. He might have restless energy and a hard body sculpted into muscle, but he was a man with a strongly sensuous streak.

Imogen gave a little shiver and clasped her hands together, trying to evict memories of his sensuality and how he'd uncovered a purely hedonistic side to her she'd never known.

'Has your family owned it long?' Her gaze drifted from the fairy-tale towers across the impressive façade.

'A couple of hundred years.'

Tension clamped her shoulders. She'd realised she was marrying into money, but the aristocracy as well? She was going to be totally out of her depth.

Not for long, reminded that persistent inner voice. The reminder dampened her momentary sense of rising panic.

The car slowed and pulled to a halt in front of the imposing building, gravel crunching under the wheels. 'Welcome to your new home, Imogen.'

Her throat clenched. He really was a man in a million. He'd taken her news with something close to equanimity, only the occasional flicker of emotion in his dark eyes betraying his shock. More, he'd not only agreed to take care of their child, he'd taken it upon himself to provide for her too.

'You didn't need to do all this.' She waved futilely. She could have been back in Sydney by now, alone. Instead, he'd brought her to his family home. That meant so much.

'Of course I do. You're carrying my child.'

Of course. His child. She had to keep remembering this was about their baby. She was just along for the ride.

Imogen bit her lip, swallowing a laugh that held no humour.

'Are you okay?' His touch on her arm was light, but she felt the imprint of his fingers in each riotously sensitive nerve ending.

'Perfect.' She turned and gave him her best smile. The one she'd practised so often before heading out to some large social event. She must be slipping, for Thierry didn't look convinced, just sat, watching, as if he read the unease and dismay she tried to hide.

'What's wrong?' Those espresso-dark eyes saw too much.

A litany of worries ran through her head. Her baby's health, her own illness, staying in France for these final months instead of Australia, where at least she spoke the language. Being a burden to Thierry and an unwelcome surprise to his family. If she wasn't careful all those concerns would submerge her just when she needed her strength.

'Neither of us really wants this marriage.' She shook her head. 'It's not what you'd planned for yourself.'

Thierry's scrutiny sharpened and his eyes narrowed. She couldn't read his expression.

'Things don't always work out the way we expect but I'm a firm believer in making the best of any situation.' His hand closed on hers, long fingers threading through hers. 'This is the right thing, Imogen. Trust me.'

CHAPTER SEVEN

IMOGEN PUT THE wicker basket down and sank onto the garden seat. Typically, it wasn't a bare stone seat. Someone had placed cushions on all the outdoor seats, in case she or Thierry or some unexpected visitor chose to stop.

Everything at the *château* was like that—not just elegant and expensive but beautifully cared for. No detail was too small, no comfort overlooked, from the scented bath oils made from herbs grown at the *château*, to crisp white sheets that smelled of sunshine and lavender from the purpose-grown drying hedge. Even the discreetly efficient lift to the top floors was hidden behind ancient panelling so as not to interfere with the ambience.

Imogen closed her eyes, soaking up the late-afternoon sunshine, enjoying the sense of utter peace. There was no sound but the drowse of bees and in the distance a motor. A car maybe, or a tractor. She inhaled, drinking in the heady scent of roses, and felt herself relax.

She'd done the right thing.

Of course she had!

It didn't matter that she felt like she'd forced Thierry into a corner so he'd been obliged to take responsibility for their child. She'd had no other option.

Nor did it matter that she was an outsider here. What mattered was doing right by her baby. If that meant spending her last months in France rather than her own country, so be it.

As if it was hard, living here at the *château*!

For days she'd rested, sleeping more than she could remember ever having done. Jeanne, the Girard's formidable cook-housekeeper, seemed to have made it her mission to tempt Imogen's appetite with one delicious treat after another. And when, with a knowing look, she'd seen Imogen turn pale at the pungent scent of fresh coffee, she'd begun providing herbal teas and delicate, light-as-air crackers that had helped settle Imogen's stomach.

Her thoughts eddied as she drifted towards sleep. It was so easy to relax here. So very peaceful.

The crunch of footsteps woke her. And the murmur of voices. Thierry's voice, a low, liquid blur of sound that flowed through her like luscious caramel pooling deep inside. Imogen kept her eyes closed just a little longer, reluctant to move. Listening to his voice was one of her greatest pleasures. Thierry could read weather forecasts or even tax law aloud and she'd melt into a puddle of pure bliss.

'Imogen?'

She opened her eyes to find him standing before her. He looked every bit as delicious as he sounded. His clothes were plain, tailored trousers and a pale shirt undone at the throat, but there was nothing ordinary about the man wearing them. He looked the epitome of hard athleticism from his solid thighs to his straight shoulders and every hard inch between.

Imogen gave a little quiver of pleasure. Every time she saw him it happened, even now. He made her silly heart stutter.

'I'd like you to meet my grandmother.' He gestured to his side, and her gaze swung to the tiny, grey-haired lady she hadn't even noticed before. A lady with a capital L, Imogen realised in the split second it took to register her immaculate hair and make-up, the sophisticated dark suit that screamed couture and the lustre of elegant pearls at her throat. She wore stockings despite the heat and gorgeous black patent shoes that Imogen wouldn't dare wear on gravel for fear of scuffing them.

Imogen shot to her feet, managing to tip over the basket of roses beside her. Secateurs clattered to the ground.

Eyes as dark as Thierry's, but much sharper, surveyed her from head to toe.

Imogen felt a flush rise to crest in her burning cheeks. She knew her shirt was rumpled, her jeans faded and one canvas shoe had got caked in mud when she'd ventured too near an ornamental pond. Faced with the other woman's elegance, Imogen felt a complete frump. It was one thing to borrow her sister's creations and play at dressing up in Paris. It was quite another to achieve that bone-deep level of stylish sophistication.

'*Bonjour*, Madame Girard.' Imogen paused, searching for the words she'd memorised: *it's very nice to meet you... 'Je suis ravie de vous rencontrer.'* Unexpected nerves made her stumble over even that simple phrase. Quickly, she put out her hand, only to whip it back when she realised she still wore gardening gloves.

'It's a pleasure to meet you at last too.' The other woman's English was crisp if heavily accented. She leaned in and kissed Imogen lightly on the cheeks in a gesture that held no discernible warmth. A light fragrance, perfectly balanced and no doubt worth a fortune, wafted around her. 'We will speak in English, as it's easier for you.'

'Thank you. I'm afraid my French is non-existent.' Under the other woman's assessing scrutiny Imogen almost blurted that she'd learned Japanese and Indonesian at school, but stopped herself before she could babble. Instead, she pulled off the soiled gloves and dropped them on the seat where Thierry had righted the basket of cut flowers.

'It's important that we become better acquainted. You have married my grandson. You are part of the family now.'

Imogen searched her inflection for any hint of welcome. She found none.

'Which is why you left *Grand-père* in Provence and hot-footed it up here,' Thierry murmured. 'It's a delightful surprise to see you.'

Fine eyebrows arched. 'He wasn't up to the journey this time.' She turned to Imogen. 'My husband has been unwell and needs rest. But we felt it important that one of us came to welcome you into the family.'

If the gleam in those shrewd eyes was any indication, it was more a matter of sizing her up. Yet who could blame the older woman?

What had Imogen expected? To be greeted by Thierry's family with open arms? She suspected she was doomed to disappointment in that case.

It didn't matter what they thought of her, she reminded herself. Unless that affected her child's future. The thought stirred Imogen's protective instincts.

'It's good of you to come all this way, Madame Girard. I'm afraid the news of our marriage must have come as a surprise to Thierry's family.'

'And presumably to your own.' Those keen eyes roved Imogen's face, as if searching for clues.

'I don't have a family.' The bald statement sounded more brutal than she'd intended and she read the shock on the older woman's face. 'I mean—'

'Sadly, Imogen recently lost her mother and her sister.' Warm fingers threaded through hers, and Imogen looked up to find Thierry watching her, his smile reassuring. His hand squeezed hers, and she smiled back gratefully. She wasn't in this alone.

Nevertheless, she felt like an imposter, pretending to be his one true love, the woman he'd spend the rest of his life with.

'I'm very sorry for your loss. That must have been very difficult.'

'Thank you. It was...difficult.' Could she sound any less sophisticated in front of this stylish matriarch?

'But now you have Thierry.'

Imogen blinked. Did his grandmother think she'd married him because she was lonely? No, more likely trapped him because of his money. 'I'm a very lucky woman.'

To her surprise, she felt Thierry's warm fingers stroke her cheek. 'I'm the lucky one, *chérie*.' His voice dropped to that low, shivery note she hadn't heard in so long. Since they'd shared a bed on her first visit to Paris. Imogen swallowed hard, hit by a surge of longing so strong she found herself swaying towards him. Yet his affectionate display was obviously a show for his grandmother. Thierry didn't want to explain the exact circumstances of their marriage and nor did she.

'You always did have luck on your side, Thierry. Now, if you'll leave us alone, I'd like to get to know your wife a little better.' It wasn't a request but an order.

Thierry ignored it. 'Let's all go inside for coffee. I've no doubt Jeanne has been busy preparing something suitable from the moment you arrived.'

Imogen liked that he wanted to look after her. But she wasn't totally helpless, even if she *had* turned to him when she hadn't known what else to do.

'We'll come in soon,' she assured him. 'It would be nice if your grandmother could show me the garden. I'm sure she knows the name of those beautiful roses at the end of the walk.' The gardener had mentioned that Madame Girard herself had overseen their planting.

'You're sure?' His eyes searched her face.

She nodded.

'Then I'll see you both inside very soon. There's a call I need to get back to.'

'Go on, Thierry.' His grandmother made a shooing motion. 'I know I interrupted your work. We'll be fine. I don't intend to eat the girl.'

As soon as he was gone Madame Girard turned to her. 'I was surprised to find him in the offices. You didn't want a honeymoon?'

She didn't beat around the bush, did she? But Imogen

rather liked that. One of the reasons she felt uncomfortable at big social events was that she'd never excelled at meaningless small talk. Those nights in Paris with Thierry were an exception, when flirting with him had been as easy as breathing.

'He has a lot of work at the moment and he can do that here.' Imogen had been surprised to discover the rear of the *château* accommodated offices for staff involved in running the Girard family's commercial interests. It was there Thierry spent his days, often working late, though always coming to share meals with her.

'Nevertheless, a bride should expect more of her husband. I'll speak with him.'

Startled, Imogen saw a flash of something like disapproval in the older woman's eyes. On her behalf?

'No! Please, don't. We're content as we are.' The thought of Thierry's grandmother telling him he had to spend more time with her…

'Content? What is that? Have you no passion, girl? No fire?'

Imogen drew herself up. 'It's not a matter of passion. It's a matter of common sense. Anyone can see Thierry has a lot on his mind right now.'

And she'd added to his burdens. It was only since she'd returned to Paris that she'd begun to realise how hard he worked. When he'd been with her before, she'd seen only the carefree side of him, the man who revelled in seeing her pleasure at her first hot-air balloon ride, or tasting her first glass of champagne.

'You're willing to take second place to business while he does so?'

'I have no complaints. Thierry has responsibilities and I knew that when we married.'

'The marriage was very sudden.' Those dark eyes glinted. 'Thierry didn't tell me exactly how long you've known each other but I don't recall him mentioning your name in the past.'

Imogen stared straight back at her interrogator. 'It was a whirlwind romance.'

'I see.' She sounded as if she didn't like what she saw. 'So, perhaps you have mutual friends. Is that how you met? You moved in the same circles?' Her gaze skated over Imogen's rumpled clothes.

Imogen held the basket close, as if that could protect her from the other woman's curiosity. If only she'd been warned of the visit, she'd have dressed up. Which was probably precisely why they'd had no warning. Thierry's grandmother struck her as a very canny woman.

'No, we don't have any mutual friends. We met by chance at a party in Paris and…'

'And he swept you off your feet?'

Imogen shrugged, ignoring the trace of a blush she felt in her cheeks. 'Something like that.' Deliberately, she held the older woman's gaze.

'I see.' Madame Girard tilted her head as if to get a better view of her. 'And your work? Do you have a job?'

Imogen's hands tightened on the basket but she drew a slow breath and released it, reminding herself it was natural Thierry's grandmother wanted to know these things. Did she think Imogen was unemployed, looking for someone to sponge off? One thing was for sure, she wouldn't mistake her for one of the idle rich, not in these clothes.

'I'm an accountant. From Australia. I was visiting Paris on holiday.'

'Where you met my grandson, had a passionate affair and found yourself pregnant.'

Imogen's breath hissed in and for a moment she felt the world wobble around her.

'Come! You need to sit.' A surprisingly firm hand gripped her upper arm, guiding her back down to the seat.

'That's better.' Madame Girard took the seat beside her. 'I don't have any patience with this fainting nonsense.'

'Good.' Imogen lifted her chin. 'Because I don't faint.'

To her amazement the other woman chuckled. The sound was unexpectedly rich and appealing. 'I'm very glad to hear it.' Then she nodded. 'With some coaching, you might even do for him very well.'

'I beg your pardon?' Imogen stared, torn between relief and offence.

'Your clothes, your lack of French… We'll have to work on both if you're to take your place beside Thierry.'

Imogen blinked at the 'we'. His grandmother intended to coach her? Or had pregnancy hormones made Imogen lose the thread of the conversation?

'How did you know I was pregnant?'

'Jeanne, of course. She's been at the *château* for years. As soon as she realised…' Madame Girard gave a fluid shrug. 'Of course she contacted me.'

'Of course.' Imogen paused, caught up in an unexpected tide of relief that she had one less secret to keep from this formidable lady. More than that, sharing the news with another woman made her feel less alone. So often she wished her mother was alive to talk to about the pregnancy. She had so many hopes and fears for this baby.

She chewed her lip. Thinking about that only made everything more difficult. Instead, she should focus on politely declining any make-over attempt. It wasn't as if she'd be here long term, so there was no question of her becoming the perfect wife for Thierry.

The knowledge stabbed, the pain sharper than before. But Imogen kept her expression neutral. She wasn't ready to share *that* with Thierry's grandmother. She already felt like she'd been stripped bare.

Curiosity got the better of her. 'You don't mind that Thierry married so quickly, or that I'm pregnant?'

'I might have, until I saw the way you looked at him.' There was a glimmer of a smile in those eyes so like Thierry's.

'The way I looked at him?'

'Absolutely. The way a woman looks when she's in love.'

Imogen gave up trying to sleep. Instead, she perched on the window seat in her bedroom.

It was twilight and in the distance she saw the haze of indigo mountains. Closer to the *château* were verdant fields and she could smell that sweet scent on the evening air again. Meadow flowers or perhaps something growing in the formal gardens. To the right was a sprinkle of lights from the nearest town.

She lifted her feet, wrapping her arms around her knees, drinking in the view.

But Madame Girard's words stole her peace.

The way a woman looks when she's in love.

Had she really looked at Thierry that way?

Imogen told herself Madame Girard indulged in wishful thinking because she wanted to see her grandson happy.

The bond between the pair had been evident through the evening they'd all spent in *madame*'s apartments—in a wing of the *château* Imogen hadn't visited before. The old lady was shrewd, with a dry sense of humour that had grown on Imogen. But sentimental? Not enough to skew her judgement.

In love.

Imogen had never been truly in love. At the time she'd thought perhaps with Scott… But, though she'd been hurt by the callous way he'd dumped her, her heart hadn't broken.

She admired Thierry. She liked him and was grateful for all he was doing for her and their child. After Scott, who'd resented the increasing time she spent with her mother as she'd faded, Imogen knew how remarkable it was to find a man who didn't run from harsh reality, but helped shoulder her burdens.

How many men would have done as Thierry had?

He wasn't content simply to put his name on the marriage contract. He was meticulous about seeing to her comfort. He never missed a meal with her and his careful attentiveness should have put her at ease.

Instead, it made her restless.

Physically she felt better than she had in weeks. But emotionally? The unwanted truth hammered at her. It wasn't her luxurious surrounds that made her edgy, or meeting Thierry's grandmother. As for her illness—she hadn't precisely become accustomed to it, but she'd learned to live in the moment as much as possible.

It was Thierry who tied her stomach in knots.

She raked her hand through her hair, pulling it back from her face.

She didn't want Thierry's hospitality. Each time he solicitously held her chair at the table or opened a door for her, impatience gnawed. He was caring and charming but there was an indefinable distance between them now.

What she wanted, what she *craved*, was his touch, his passion. Not love, she assured herself, but intimacy.

When she'd had that in Paris she'd felt able to cope with the future. In some inexplicable way it had given her the strength to face what was to come. Even after all this time she still reached for him in the night, waking to a loneliness even more desolate for his absence.

Had his attraction for her been so short-lived? Or did her illness turn him off? Or her pregnancy?

Or did he hold back from her for some other reason?

A breeze wafted through the window, stirring her nightdress against her breasts and teasing her bare arms. Her eyelids flickered as she thought of Thierry and how sensitive she'd been to his lightest touch. He'd made her body come alive as never before. He'd awakened something in her that refused to go back into hibernation.

A sound drew her attention to the door connecting her room to Thierry's.

Imogen's lips firmed. She wasn't dead yet.

Thierry paused in the act of hauling off his shirt when he heard a tap on his door. Not the door to his private sitting room but the one connecting to Imogen's room. The one he'd tried to ignore since they'd arrived, knowing she slept just metres away.

He'd almost locked it so he couldn't be tempted to do something reprehensible like forget the state of her health and take what he hungered for.

He let his shirt drop back into place, even doing up some of the buttons again, which was when he noticed the tremor in his hands.

'Thierry?'

He swung around. The door was ajar, and Imogen stood there, her hair tumbling about her shoulders and breasts in shining waves of ebony.

His gut clenched and a hammering started up in his chest. It took a split second to realise it was his heart, throbbing to an urgent new beat.

'Are you okay?' He paced towards her then pulled up short. He needed distance. That pale nightdress revealed too much. Her nipples pressed, proud and erect, against the light fabric and his palms tingled as he remembered how they felt, budding in his hands. How they tasted, sweet as sugar syrup and warm woman on his tongue.

He tried but couldn't stop his gaze skating lower to the hint of the darkness at the apex of her thighs. Thierry swallowed at the memories of her naked in his bed. His lower body turned into cast metal. A film of sweat broke out across his brow and his throat turned desert dry.

'What's wrong?' His voice was hoarse. 'Do you need a doctor?'

She shook her head and, mesmerised, he watched the way those dark locks slid and separated around her pouting breasts. He knew Imogen had a body to please a man. It was only now, worn down by the weight of abstinence, that he realised it could torture just as well.

Never had he been as fervently eager for work as he had been since their wedding. He was actually grateful for the distraction it gave from his wife.

'No, I'm not sick.' Her words had that throaty edge she got when nervous or aroused. Adrenalin shot through him, and he had a battle not to cross the room and haul her close. Of course she wasn't aroused. 'I wanted to talk.'

'Talk?' The last thing he needed was an intimate chat here in his bedroom. 'Can it wait till tomorrow?'

She shook her head and his breathing stalled as he watched her hair caress and frame her beautiful breasts.

Resolutely, he reminded himself that Imogen now fitted under the category of 'duty'. She and their child were his responsibility. He couldn't let himself be distracted by selfish cravings when he had a duty to care for them both. He'd spent years in the pursuit of pleasure. He could be utterly single-minded when it came to doing what he wanted. He couldn't afford to lose focus now and give in to the urge for pleasure. He needed control, purpose, resolve.

Besides, he didn't like the morass of emotions that threatened whenever he thought of Imogen the woman, rather than Imogen his responsibility. He didn't deal in emotion, except for the frustrations and elations of his chosen sports.

'Now's not the time, Imogen. It's late.' He watched her stiffen and silently cursed his harsh tone.

He shoved his hands in his trouser pockets. As if that made it easier to resist the temptation to touch! An ache started in his jaw from clenching his teeth too tight.

'What's bothering you? Is it *Grand-mère*? I know she can be overwhelming at first but she likes you.'

'You can tell that?'

He nodded. 'I think she liked the way you spoke your mind. She isn't one for prevarication.'

'So I gathered.' Imogen gnawed the corner of her bottom lip, and he wanted to reach out and stop her.

'She offended you?'

'No. I rather liked her too, though she made me feel like a fashion disaster.'

'No one expects you to dress up all the time.' Imogen in high heels and that red, clingy dress was branded too clearly on his brain for anything like comfort. It had kept him awake too many nights. Besides, he liked her in jeans; liked the way they shaped her long legs and…

'Just as well.' Something like hurt glowed in her hazel eyes. 'I feel like a fraud going along with her plans to improve me.'

'She means well. And a tutor to help you with French is an excellent idea. I should have thought of it myself.'

'It's not that. I'd like to learn French.' Her gaze slid from his then back. The impact of those eyes on his should have knocked him back on his feet. There was so much *feeling* there. It was like looking into her soul. 'I just don't feel right, pretending I'm your wife for real.'

'You are my wife. Believe me, the ceremony was legally binding, even if it was brief.'

'But I'm not the woman who's going to be with you for the rest of your days. This is a temporary arrangement for my benefit.'

Thierry had never wanted a woman to be with him for the rest of his days. Not since Sandrine. But he couldn't say that to a woman whose life was measured in months rather than years. The truth was he'd do whatever it took to make her remaining time as easy as possible.

He didn't just lust after Imogen. He didn't just see her as a responsibility. He cared about her.

Which meant he had to keep his focus on her well-being.

'Don't forget the child is mine too. We're in this together, Imogen.'

A little of the tension eased from her features, and he was stunned at how good it felt that he'd been able to do that for her.

'You don't have to worry about anything.' He kept his voice soothing. 'I'll take care of everything.' He paused, wondering whether to tell her his news.

'What is it?' She moved away from the door, her nightgown drifting around her like temptation.

'Sorry?'

'There's something you're not saying.'

Thierry frowned. Since when had she been able to read him? He prided himself on his ability to keep his thoughts to himself.

'Nothing to worry about.' But he saw she didn't believe him. Perhaps she'd had so much bad news she now expected the worst. 'Just that I've managed to get you an appointment with one of the country's finest specialists. They're sending to Australia for your medical records.'

'I see.' Her mouth twisted, and he wanted to reach out and smooth those plump lips with his thumb, stroke her hair and tell her everything would be all right. But the hell of it was he couldn't.

'That's very good of you. Thanks.' The huskiness had gone from her voice, leaving it flat.

Thierry's muscles bunched as he fought the urge to reach for her. His embrace might soothe her temporarily but at the risk of him taking things too far. And her fragility was for once obvious in her delicate features.

'Was there anything else you wanted to talk about? My *grand-mère*, perhaps?'

'No. I just…' She paused so long he began to wonder what was wrong.

In a flurry of lace and cotton she crossed the floor, planting her hands on his tense shoulders. She was so close he felt her like the earth felt the sun, drawn to her magnetic warmth. Her lashes lifted to reveal eyes of sherry-brown spangled with green that made him think of mountain streams and ecstasy. She cupped the back of his head, narrow fingers sliding through his hair, sending rivers of molten energy straight to his groin.

'I needed to thank you.' She opened her mouth as if to say more then shut it again, her gaze zeroing on his mouth.

An instant later she'd risen on her toes, leaning in so her breasts pushed, soft and enticing, against him. Her lips were hot and sweet on his, seeking, torturing with the promise of delight.

A quake rocked him to the soles of his feet. His hands fisted in his pockets so hard he thought they might never loosen again. He breathed in her scent, tasting her on his lips, and almost lost his resolve. He wanted this so badly. He wanted so much more than he should if he was to look after her as she deserved.

A lifetime's experience in giving in to temptation had him dragging his hands out of his pockets, anchoring them at her sides where he felt the supple shift of toned muscle and the mind-destroying seduction of her in-curving waist.

Something like a growl erupted from the back of his throat and her tiny, answering moan just about undid him. All he had to do was open his mouth and…

With a surge of inexplicable strength he put her from him, stepping back so he held her at arm's length. His arms were shaking and his heart galloped out of control, but he'd done it. By the skin of his teeth he'd actually done what he should have done all along. She didn't have to thank him with the gift of her body. A better man wouldn't have countenanced it even for a second.

'There's no need to thank me, Imogen.' He barely recognised his voice as finally he managed to drag his hands away. 'Not like this.'

Something flashed in her eyes. Something swift and raw that he felt like a smack to the face. But it was gone in a second. Her flushed features set in an expression he couldn't read. Her lips were slightly parted as she dragged in air, and her hazel eyes looked past him as if the far wall fascinated her.

'Truly, Imogen, there's no need for that sort of thanks.'

Slowly, she nodded, then before he realised what she was about she was walking out the door, leaving his hands empty. 'I understand. Goodnight, Thierry.'

CHAPTER EIGHT

IMOGEN SAT STRAIGHT in her seat, braced for bad news. Hope for the best but prepare for the worst, wasn't that the adage? Right now she was hoping the doctor would confirm her child would be safe. The alternative…

A callused hand enclosed hers, long fingers gripping gently.

Startled, she looked around to Thierry beside her. He was watching the doctor pore over her scan results, yet he'd sensed her fear as if attuned to her.

He'd done that before, she remembered, the day his grandmother had arrived. His gentle touch on her cheek then had calmed her, made her feel he was on her side.

Imogen released a shivery breath, trying to find a place of calm amongst her whirling emotions.

Thierry's touch was a two-edged sword. Unashamedly she clung to his hand, grateful for the reminder she wasn't alone. Yet the poignancy of his touch lacerated something fragile inside. He hadn't touched her willingly since that day with his grandmother in the garden. The night she'd gone to him, eager to show how much she needed him, he'd stood aloof.

The memory of his beautiful, big body, so still and unresponsive when she'd offered herself to him, gouged at far more than her self-respect. It felt as if she'd swallowed a razor blade that cut her every time she breathed. The pain of his rejection rivalled even her blinding headaches at their worst.

Had she really invested so much in this man?

Imogen looked away to the framed diplomas on the wall.

Thierry hadn't even bothered to take his hands out of

his pockets that night she'd kissed him! So much for rekindling the passion they'd shared. He'd stood there, enduring her touch, till finally he'd grabbed her and put her aside. No words could have made it clearer that for him the physical side of their relationship was dead.

She really had been a temporary fling.

'Imogen?' His low voice curled around her, beckoning, but she refused to turn. She had to hold herself together.

'Madame Girard.' At last the doctor spoke. Imogen squared her shoulders in preparation for the inevitable.

Yet, instead of the grave expression doctors usually reserved for delivering bad news, this man looked animated. Pleased. Her breath caught. Did that mean her baby would be okay? Involuntarily, her fingers clenched around Thierry's.

'You're something of a puzzle, Madame Girard.' The doctor shook his head slowly but there was no mistaking the hint of a smile at the corners of his mouth.

'I am?' Her voice was a husk of sound.

'Your symptoms fit a classic pattern and, combined with your family history…' He spread his hands as if to say there was nothing he could do for her.

Her heart dived and she bit down a gasp of distress.

A chair scraped and Thierry roped a long arm around her shoulders. Warmth enveloped her, the woodsy scent of the outdoors and something more, something beyond mere physical comfort. She leaned into him. No matter that she could do this alone if she had to. She'd never been more grateful for company in her life, even if it came from the man who saw her solely as a form of duty.

'Despite that, I'm pleased to tell you the headaches and vision problems aren't what you think.'

'Pardon?'

The doctor smiled, his eyes alight. 'Contrary to expectations, you're not suffering the same disease as your mother.'

The air rushed from her lungs as if from a punctured balloon. 'I'm not?'

'Absolutely not. In fact, I can tell you there is no tumour, malignant or otherwise.' His smile became a beam.

Dazed, Imogen shook her head. 'I don't understand.'

'There was never a tumour, though it seems your general practitioner, like you, feared the worst.' He spoke slowly, glancing again at the test results. 'I've consulted with both your family doctor and my specialist colleague in Australia. The one you were supposed to see but didn't.'

She didn't miss the questioning inflection in his voice, or the tightening of Thierry's grip on her shoulder.

'There didn't seem much point. I knew what he was going to say. I just…' She looked up into surprisingly sympathetic grey eyes and found the words tumbling out. 'I couldn't bear facing the diagnosis so soon after losing my mother. I felt trapped.' She hefted a deep breath into too-tight lungs. 'I decided to get away, just for a while, before I had to face all that.' She waved a hand at the reports on his desk. 'But you're saying it's not a tumour? What is it, then?'

'I understand from your family doctor that you also lost your sister recently?'

Imogen could have howled with impatience. Why didn't he just tell her what was wrong with her?

Thierry's warm hand caressed her shoulder in a gesture of support that helped her gather her scattered wits.

'That's right. She died suddenly in an accident.'

'And then your mother became ill?'

Imogen nodded. 'Very soon afterwards. But I don't see how that's relevant.'

Sympathetic grey eyes held hers. 'Stress and grief can do amazing things, Madame Girard.'

'I don't understand.' She leaned forward, dislodging Thierry's grip. 'Please, just tell me what's going on.'

'I'm pleased to say that, on the basis of these very extensive tests, there's nothing physically wrong with you.'

'But that can't be! I'm not imagining those headaches. They're so bad they even affect my vision.'

The doctor nodded. 'I'm sure they are. Tell me, are they still as frequent?'

Imogen hesitated, calculating. 'No, not as often as before.' She spoke slowly. 'I haven't had one since Paris.' She couldn't remember the exact date and darted a sideways glance at Thierry but he wasn't looking at her. His attention was fixed on the doctor.

'So you're saying all this is the result of stress?' Thierry's voice held a note of disbelief that matched her own. 'There's no physical cause?'

'That doesn't make the pain any less real. I have no doubt the symptoms your wife has experienced were every bit as disturbing as ones caused by a tumour.' He looked down at his notes then up at Imogen. 'It seems to me that you've been through a very traumatic time, Madame Girard. The best remedy is rest, and…' a small smile played at his mouth '…something positive in your life. Like a baby to look forward to.'

'You're serious?' Imogen couldn't take it in.

'Absolutely. The symptoms you're experiencing will pass with time.'

A great hiccupping sob rose in her throat, and she crossed her arms around her middle, folding in on herself as shock detonated at her core. Through a blur of emotion she heard the doctor reassure her, telling her he'd be happy to see her again if she had any questions later, and more that she didn't really take in.

All she registered was that she was okay. She and her baby were going to live. Everything would be all right.

And one other detail. The fact that Thierry hadn't touched her again. She missed the warmth of his large, reassuring hand.

'I feel like such a fool,' she said again, watching the streets pass by as Thierry drove them out of the city. 'I just can't believe it. It seems so incredible.'

Thierry didn't say anything. When she turned to look, his profile was set in lines of concentration, his brow furrowed and his mouth firm.

The traffic was heavy, she told herself. Of course he needed to focus on that. Even to her own ears she sounded like a broken record, replaying the same phrases again and again. But she needed to talk about this to make it real. It was so unexpected, so much the miracle she'd never dared hope for, that she couldn't quite believe it.

Her palm covered her belly and gratitude overcame her. Her baby would be all right. She felt the weight of every anxious night ease from her shoulders as tears pricked her eyes. She let her head sink back against the headrest, relief vying with so many other emotions she couldn't get a grip on.

Just as well it was Thierry driving. She wouldn't have trusted herself.

'I still don't believe it,' she murmured. 'The one and only time I act on impulse.' She clasped her hands together. 'All my life I've been cautious, the one who never acted rashly, always considering the pros and cons before making a decision. Yet that one time I acted on the spur of the moment…'

That day in the Sydney waiting room, defeat had pressed down so hard, there'd seemed no room for doubt. She'd *known* she had the same fatal illness as her mother. 'I should have stayed for that appointment instead of haring off to the other side of the globe.'

But if you had, you'd never have met Thierry. You wouldn't be expecting this child.

Shocking as it was to find herself pregnant, Imogen couldn't wish that undone.

She turned and peeked at Thierry through her lashes. His jaw was hard-set, emphasising the strong thrust of his nose and the slashing lines of his cheekbones.

She dragged in a rough breath that didn't fill her lungs.

'All of this…us…' she waved her hand '…is because I acted impulsively. I should have waited and checked my facts.'

Still he said nothing.

'I'm sorry, Thierry. Truly sorry. You must be upset.'

'You think I'd prefer if the doctor had confirmed today that you're dying?' A muscle twitched in his jaw. 'What sort of man do you think I am? You think I'm upset that you're going to live?' Finally, he looked her way, his gaze piercing. 'What have I done to give you such an opinion of me?'

'You know what I mean. If I hadn't jumped to conclusions all this wouldn't have happened. We wouldn't be married. Because of that mistake, we're stuck with each other.'

Unless, of course, they divorced. But for the life of her she couldn't bring herself to mention it. Not yet. Not till she'd had time to absorb everything.

'What's done is done, Imogen. There's nothing to be gained in lashing yourself over it.'

'You think not?' Imogen stared. He seemed far too calm, though now she looked properly, the chiselled stillness of his profile hinted at fierce control. What was he holding back?

'I didn't do it deliberately.' She reached out and placed her palm on his thigh. Instantly, she felt the long muscle beneath her hand bunch tight and solid.

It was the first time she'd reached for him since that night in her room. Imogen looked at her pale hand against the taut, dark fabric of his trousers and wondered with a catch in her chest whether it would be the last time. 'You have to believe me. I wasn't lying or trying to trick you. I truly believed—'

'You think I don't know that?' Again, Thierry's gaze captured hers, shooting fire along veins turned frosty with shock.

'I don't know what you believe.' Thierry had been so good to her, so supportive, but she'd never been able to read him fully except when they shared pleasure. Right now he was giving a good imitation of a graven image. She felt none of the closeness she'd experienced before. She lifted her hand, warm from touching him, and tucked it into her lap.

'Your shock was obvious when the doctor told you the truth. I thought for a moment you might faint.'

Yet he hadn't wrapped his arm around her and hauled her close as he'd done before.

'I believe…' He paused and she could have sworn her heartbeat slowed in expectation. 'That, instead of apologising, you need to celebrate. It's not often a dying woman gets such a reprieve.'

Finally, his mouth curled up at the corner, and Imogen's heart gave a flutter of relief. It took a while to notice the tension in his neck and jaw hadn't eased.

They celebrated with lunch at the sort of restaurant Imogen had read about in guide books but never anticipated visiting. The service was impeccable, the food unlike anything she'd ever tasted and the ambience discreetly elegant. If the wine waiter was surprised they toasted her news with sparkling water, he didn't show it.

Thierry was charming, urbane and witty and, by the time the chef came out to greet them, Imogen felt more relaxed than she had in ages.

It was as she was coming back from the ladies' room that she saw Thierry in conversation with another diner, a fit-looking man with a shock of shaggy blond hair.

'A friend?' she asked as she sat down, watching the stranger walk out the door.

It struck her that she didn't know Thierry's friends. They'd spent all their time together, unless Thierry was working, as he did so many hours in the day.

'Yes, someone from the old days.'

'The old days?' She wished she'd returned to the table sooner.

'The days before I became a respectable businessman.' It should have been a joke but it didn't sound like it.

She tilted her head to one side. 'What did you do before you became respectable?'

'Whatever I pleased.' When he saw her watching, he continued. 'Skiing, parties, trekking, ballooning, more parties.' He swallowed the last of his coffee. 'In fact, I was just invited to a weekend climbing in the Alps.'

'And are you going?'

He shrugged, but she didn't miss the glitter in his eyes. It was the same look she'd seen when he'd told her about some of his far-flung adventures. 'I have too much to do. Too many responsibilities.'

You're one of those responsibilities.

You relied on him when you were desperate and look where that got you both—trapped in a marriage that should never have happened.

'I think you should go.' Imogen wasn't aware of formulating the words but suddenly they were emerging from her mouth.

'Pardon?'

'Look at the hours you work.' He might be meticulous about joining her for meals but he was usually back at work in the evening. When did he get time off? He'd made time in Paris but now his business seemed to consume most of his waking hours. That and being on hand for her.

'That's because I've got deadlines.'

'Can't they be put back a few days? Long enough for a short break?' She watched his eyes narrow on the coffee cup he twisted with one hand. 'Surely nothing will go wrong if you take a weekend off? What are two days?'

Besides, it would do her good to have a few days alone. She had a lot of thinking to do. After months getting used to the idea of dying, she had to get her head around the notion of living.

Then there was this situation they were in—man and wife in a marriage that now had no built-in end date. Marriage to a man who was protective and caring but no longer desired her.

'You should go,' she urged, her constricting throat making her voice husky.

'Two days,' he mused, frowning. 'I admit, it's tempting.'

Two days turned into four. In fact, it would be five by the time he returned. Tonight was his fourth night away.

After the freedom of the mountains, the thrill of pitting himself against the elements on some of the region's most treacherous climbs, Thierry had been only too ready to agree when his friends had suggested an extra night at the resort before returning to his normal life.

Yet maybe he was getting too old for this. The hot shower tonight had been bliss on his sorely tried body. He couldn't remember feeling this level of weariness after a few days' climbing. Or maybe he felt out of sorts because he still grappled with the bizarre soap-opera storyline his life had become.

He swirled his cognac, inhaling its rich aroma, then knocked it back in one. The shot of heat to his belly was satisfyingly definite, unlike so much in his life now. He looked up, ignoring the party going on around him, and caught the bartender's eye, gesturing for another.

Thierry rolled his shoulders but couldn't shift the tension that had settled there. The sense of being weighed down. But worse was the roiling morass of *feelings*.

Thierry grimaced. His life had been simple and perfect. Yes, he'd had a little heartbreak in his youth but that had merely left him able to play the field, enjoying freedom in the bedroom as well as in his sports. Even the yoke of the family business hadn't taken that away from him. He'd shouldered massive burdens but he was close to freeing himself of that.

His old life had beckoned. Until Imogen.

He lifted his glass and slugged back another mouthful, ignoring the fact this liquor deserved slow appreciation. He didn't have the patience for that. He needed something to cut through the web of emotions tangling his brain.

He'd never felt such relief in his life as when the doctor had said Imogen was safe. That she and the baby would live. But the news hadn't just brought relief.

Cool logic told him Imogen hadn't deliberately set out to trap him into marriage. He'd been the one to persuade her and there'd been no mistaking her utter shock at the doctor's pronouncement. It wasn't her fault.

Damn it all, he could even sympathise with her walking out of that Sydney waiting room and heading for adventure rather than facing more appointments and treatment. It was the sort of thing he could imagine himself doing.

Yet no amount of logic could shift the sensation that he'd got caught in a net, in a situation far more complex than he'd anticipated. Marrying for the sake of a child was one thing. Acquiring a long-term wife was another. Then there were these feelings that clogged his chest. Half-formed ideas and sensations that were totally unfamiliar.

Thierry wanted his simple life back. Even in the beginning when he'd had to work soul-destroying hours to salvage the business he'd been certain of his purpose, and what little free time he'd had was his own to use as he chose.

Now he felt tethered. Tangled. Worse, he felt… He didn't know what he felt. Just that he didn't like it.

After the wedding he'd put Imogen in that box labelled 'duty'. He'd been able to deal with her as his responsibility when she was off-limits. Now suddenly that label didn't fit and all sorts of insidious ideas were weaving their way through his brain.

The waiter returned, and Thierry gestured for him to leave the bottle. Helping himself, he poured a double. His mouth twisted. He never drank this much. He preferred to keep his wits about him. But that hadn't done much good lately. Maybe he'd find clarity this way. *Something* had to break this untenable bind he found himself in.

He'd lost count of his drinks when he heard a husky whisper beside him. 'Is there enough for me to have a sip?'

He turned and for a second the edges of his vision blurred. But he had no trouble focusing on the woman beside him. Tall, slim, with cornflower-blue eyes and hair the colour of sunlight. Her mouth was wide and her expression aware. Exactly the sort of beautiful woman he'd always preferred. Given her height, he guessed she had long, lissom legs.

Thierry smiled and her pout of enquiry turned into a smile that would have melted the snow off Mont Blanc.

She put a glass on the bar, and he swiped up the cognac bottle, pouring her a measure without spilling a drop. He was congratulating himself on that feat when she leaned in to pick up her drink, pressing against him from breast to knee.

He felt the subtle stretch and arch of her body as she knocked back her drink, her breasts thrusting into his torso. Heat shot through him at that deliberate invitation.

She put her glass down and, holding his eyes, slowly licked her lips. Her bottom lip shimmered, and Thierry felt a pounding in his head—or was it his chest?—as she slid her arms around his neck.

'How about a private party?' she whispered, her breath tickling his throat.

Then she reached up, pressing her mouth to his, and he found his hands clamping convulsively around her waist.

CHAPTER NINE

THIERRY DROVE ROUND to the offices at the back of the *château*.

He wasn't really in a fit state for work but there'd be crucial matters for his attention after five days away. Two property deals were nearing conclusion and he wanted an update. Plus there'd be the revised schedule for the new ski resort to check.

Besides, he wasn't ready to face his wife.

Wife. That word had become real in ways he'd never imagined when he and Imogen had married in that swift civil ceremony.

A wife was more than a temporary responsibility, a woman to be cared for in her hour of need.

Imogen had ceased being a responsibility and had again become a woman—with all the complications that entailed. Not a woman for a quick liaison but a woman with whom his life was now inextricably entangled.

Because he'd followed his instinct and decided on marriage. He'd spent his life acting on instinct, even in business, and it rarely let him down.

His mouth set. There was always a first time.

He parked and switched off the ignition. His head beat like a drum, the pounding an insistent, punishing beat reminding him how foolish he'd been last night.

As if alcohol would solve his problems! Not even climbing, one of his favourite sports, had cleared his mind. Instead of enjoying the challenge of the sport, he'd been distracted by thoughts of Imogen and the disturbing emotions she stirred.

As for that debacle in the bar last night!

He leaned back against the headrest, shoving his hand through his hair.

Even drunk, he'd known what the blonde wanted. How could he not? He was the master of the short-term affair.

Too much cognac was a convenient excuse for the fact he'd smiled right back and offered her a drink. As if tangling with one sexy woman would solve the problems he had with another!

He couldn't remember if he'd felt a sizzle of anticipation as she'd sidled up to him, or what, if anything, had gone through his brain. All he knew was, the moment she'd pressed her mouth to his, revulsion had knifed him. Revulsion at her touch and, more, at himself.

His hands hadn't been gentle as he'd shoved her away. He had a suspicion she might even bear bruises from his touch, though last night she'd looked too shocked to register pain.

Thierry scrubbed a hand over his face. It had just been a kiss, a split second of a kiss at that, yet for the first time in his life he'd felt guilty about being with a woman.

Guilt and anger, and that sick swirl in his belly he'd like to believe was the result of too much alcohol. Instead, he suspected it was due to something else entirely.

Shoving the car door open, he swung out, letting it slam, and strode to the offices. He needed an afternoon concentrating on reports, plans and the delicate power play of property negotiations. Anything to take his mind off personal matters.

He made it past most of the offices and had reached the threshold of his own when someone called his name.

Thierry paused, biting down an oath. He wanted privacy, but this was why he was here, to lead the team. He turned and saw one of the legal staff approaching, an envelope in his hand and an expression on his face that had Thierry instantly alert.

'Is there a problem?' Mentally, he flicked through the

current investments—commercial property, high-end resorts, the Côte du Rhône vineyard and—

'No problem.' Yet the lawyer's smile looked forced. 'Just tying up loose ends.' He offered the envelope and, to Thierry's surprise, walked quickly away.

Thierry's fingers tingled as he surveyed it. His staff here made a close-knit team, without the formality of the Paris office. They were relaxed and friendly, even in times of high workload. But his senior legal advisor was worried.

Thierry entered his office and shut the door. He strode to the window and slid the contents of the envelope into his hand.

It was just a few pages. Flicking to the back, he saw Imogen's name and signature and a date two days ago, all witnessed. Thierry frowned and flipped to the front.

Minutes later he stood, staring, his hand carving through his hair to clutch his scalp. Dimly, he registered a cramping in his chest that reminded him to suck in air.

This was what his legal staff had done while he'd been away?

The paper crackled as it crumpled in his fist.

Imogen must have asked them to draw this up. No one else would have dared consider it.

He dragged in another breath and searched for calm. It eluded him. Why had she so ostentatiously cut herself off from his wealth, the material support he could provide? It should have felt like a reprieve yet in some obscure way it was a slap in the face, made more insulting because of the shame he felt after last night.

He told himself a single kiss with a stranger didn't taint his honour, yet he felt…stained. It had to be because of this indignity Imogen had engineered. No doubt his employees were gossiping about the fiasco their boss's marriage had become. Thierry had never in his life cared about gossip, but to be made a laughing stock in his own home…

The papers fell as he marched across the room, wrenched open the door and strode out.

She wasn't in her room. A scan revealed nothing except her passport on the dresser beside her purse.

Thierry scowled. Why was her passport out?

The sound of running water penetrated and he stalked to the bathroom door, pushed it open and walked in.

Behind the clear glass of the shower screen, water sluiced down Imogen's lush body. Her head arched back as she massaged shampoo from her long hair. The pose thrust her breasts out, silhouetting them against the window beyond.

Thierry stilled, his hand on the door knob. Everything inside him collapsed in on itself. Arousal, strong as the tug of the ocean's inexorable current, dragged at his lower body. He didn't notice the pounding in his head any more, just his lungs' short, sharp grabs for oxygen and the thunder of his heartbeat rapping his ribs.

'Thierry?' Her eyes opened wide, and she stood transfixed, glistening and perfect. His gaze traced her raspberry-pink nipples that beaded as he watched, down the plane of her ribcage to her taut belly that showed no sign yet of his child inside.

His child.

His hand tightened on the door as she turned her back to wrench off the taps. The dip and curve of her glistening back was entrancing.

His wife.

The thought curled through him like a beckoning finger, inviting him into the room.

He scooped up a towel and pulled open the shower door. Amazingly, she crossed one arm over her breasts as she turned, her other hand covering her pubic area. As if he didn't recall every slick curve and plane of that gorgeous body!

That was the problem. All this time dealing with Imogen the duty rather than Imogen the sensuous woman had left him sleep-deprived. No wonder he was out of sorts.

'There's no need for modesty, *ma chère*.'

Her chin tilted and something hot jabbed through him. He'd always responded to a challenge.

'I'd prefer you to knock before you come in.'

'It's late for setting ground rules, Imogen. You're my wife and I have a right to be here.' The long walk through the *château* had fuelled his roaring indignation.

His eyes flicked down, taking in her pale skin, blush-pink from the shower, and her sinuous curves.

Reason and patience retreated. He was tired of being patient. More, he was tired of the bitter stew of emotions he couldn't banish. Emotions Imogen had created.

He didn't do emotion. Not with women.

He should have followed through that night she'd kissed him in his bedroom. She wouldn't be tying him in knots if he had. But telling himself his frustration levels were his own fault didn't help. He'd needed that mental and physical distance to keep himself sane and ensure he looked after her as she deserved.

Mouth setting in a crooked line, she snatched the towel from him. He had one last glimpse of tip-tilted breasts jiggling deliciously before she wrapped the massive bath sheet around her, even covering her shoulders, as if knowing how her bare skin inflamed him.

She stared straight back, her look all hauteur, as if he'd crawled out of a Marseilles sewer.

Instead of freezing him, that stare ignited something dangerous. Thierry felt it like a whoosh of flame, razing his carefully nurtured restraint.

No woman looked at him like that. Ever. Especially not the woman for whom he'd done so much!

Thierry's hands were hard and brown against the white towel as he grabbed her shoulders. He felt her fine bones, heard the flurry of her quickened breathing, and that sent fiery heat spilling through his veins.

'What did you think you were doing, drawing up that… that…?' Indignation stole his vocabulary.

'That post-nuptial agreement?' Her chin notched.

'Were you deliberately trying to insult me?'

Her eyes widened. 'Of course not. I don't see the problem.'

'You go to my staff and ask them to draw up a contract specifying you renounce any claim to my assets, weeks *after* we marry. You sign in front of witnesses, and you don't see a problem?' His voice rose and beneath his hold she flinched.

Good! How dared she make him an object of ridicule?

Yet if anything her mouth set tighter. Green fire sparked in her eyes.

'I was doing you a favour. Your lawyers thought so. You should have seen their relief when I explained what I wanted.'

'You think I live my life to please lawyers?' His fingers clamped harder.

'I was doing the right thing.' Her chin jutted and her brilliant eyes met his unerringly. 'You didn't want a permanent wife. If you had, I'm sure you'd have expected a pre-nup. Circumstances have changed and I wanted you to know I'm not hanging around, aiming for a share of your wealth.'

Not hanging around? Was that why her passport was out? Warning jangled, and Thierry yanked her body full against his, soft to his rigid frame. He let go of her shoulders and wrapped his arms around her, pinioning her.

Memory assaulted him. Of that woman last night, her body pressed to his, her lips against his mouth. And all he felt was disgust. Because she hadn't been Imogen.

It was his wife he wanted. No one else.

That truth had hammered at him all day. There'd been no evading it, no matter how he'd tried.

Imogen had burrowed under his skin, destroying his interest in other women. That was bad enough. Worse was the fact she now acted as if she didn't want him! She deliberately provoked.

'What did I ever do to suggest I believed you were after my money?' His words were sharp as a lash, and he felt her tense. He breathed deep, nostrils flaring as he dragged in the scent of damp, sweet woman. 'When have I *ever* insulted you as you've insulted me? You make me look like a mercenary, gullible fool, scared you're going to fleece me. A man who needs saving from his own decisions!'

'That wasn't my intention.' Her eyes widened. This close, he caught the shock in those sherry-brown depths.

'You think I'm so incompetent I need protecting from my actions?'

'I think you're overreacting.' Her finger jabbed his chest. 'I saw your expression after the doctor said I wasn't ill. I saw your doubts.' She tried to stare him down. 'You were wondering if I'd deliberately misled you, weren't you? You suspected I was some gold-digger who'd set up an elaborate scam.'

Fury spiked in Thierry's gut, because for a split second the question *had* surfaced. That was what his lawyer had warned. But Thierry had dismissed the idea. Instead, he'd trusted her, ignoring any such doubt as unworthy.

How many men would have done that?

Besides, Imogen's reaction at the doctor's news had been absolutely genuine.

'What you saw was shock,' he ground out between clenched teeth. 'You'll pardon me for that, given everything that went before. Or are you the only one allowed to be taken by surprise?'

'It was more than surprise. You were quiet. You weren't...' For a split second he'd have sworn he read vulnerability in her expression but then she shoved her finger into his chest again, as if *he* were at fault.

He, who'd done nothing but look after her from the start!

'Weren't what?' he growled.

She shook her head and a slick ribbon of dark hair slid over her shoulder. 'You're saying you weren't regretting this marriage? You weren't regretting *me*?'

'You think I'd rather the doctor had confirmed you were dying? *That's* what you think of me?'

Deliberately, he lashed his anger higher, ignoring the fact there was a grain of truth in her words—he'd never expected to have a real marriage, only a short-term solution to the problem of caring for Imogen and her child.

Her eyes held his. 'Why are you so angry, Thierry?' Her breath came in short bursts that pushed her breasts against his torso and sent need quaking through him. Being close to her spun him out till he teetered on the brink of control. 'I don't understand. I was trying to do the right thing, making it clear I didn't expect more from you.'

He stared down at the mutinous line of her mouth. The mix of anger and hurt in her eyes.

Why *was* he angry?

What she said made sense. Yet he didn't want that sort of favour. At some deep, primitive level her action carved at his honour, his masculine pride.

Was it the careless way she spurned the fortune he'd worked like a slave to secure that needled? Or that he couldn't conquer the unfamiliar mix of emotions she'd stirred?

Or was it that the gesture felt like a rejection of *him*?

He hadn't known rejection since he was twenty and Sandrine had chosen another man. Since then he'd ensured his liaisons were short and easy, ones he could walk away from without a backward glance. Always he was in control—the hunter, the seducer, the one to leave.

The thought of Imogen spurning him made him wild.

The fire spread from his belly, coursing out in molten waves.

'Why have you got your passport out?'

She blinked. 'I wondered if I should book a flight to Australia. Clearly, you're not going to want me here long term.'

'Clearly?'

Her eyes skated away from his, and he felt something loosen inside.

'I don't belong here, Thierry. That's obvious.'

He ignored the strange, queasy sensation her words provoked. 'You were going to run away?'

Her gaze met his again in a clash that should have struck sparks. 'Of course not. I was waiting till you came home to talk about it.' For the first time he read hesitation in her expression. 'Now you're here we can discuss it. Just give me time to get dressed.' She gripped the towel tighter and made to take a step back. But he didn't let her go. Instead, his arms closed hard around her.

Imogen's head jerked up, consternation battling something he couldn't identify in her expression.

Why was she worried? She wasn't afraid of him. She'd made that clear. She was ready to walk out on him.

'No.' The word emerged from his tight throat. 'You're not going anywhere.'

She scowled and shoved her hands against his chest as if to push him away. The movement shifted the towel, revealing a tempting sliver of peachy, pale skin. 'What's wrong with you, Thierry? I don't understand.'

Nor did he. That made his anger burn brighter. The fact that it was instinctive, uncontrollable, totally inexplicable.

He just knew that none of this was right.

He'd be damned if he'd let her leave before he worked it out.

'Then understand this.' Hauling her to him, he took her mouth in a swooping kiss that started as punishing but morphed in a heartbeat to urgent, hungry, demanding. Desperate.

A moment's hesitation, a stillness that made something like fear rise in him, then her lips opened beneath his like a fragile blossom responding to sunlight.

This was what he wanted. What he'd craved. Imogen's fragrance, her taste, invaded his senses, a sweet, addictive flavour that blasted the back off his head as she tentatively moved her mouth against his.

One arm lashed about her waist and his other roved up to cup the back of her neck, supporting her as he bowed her back. She clung to his shirt and he knew a surge of triumph.

A shudder racked her, and he felt it from his mouth, down all the places where their bodies melded, right to the soles of his feet, braced wide to support them both. His brain told him to pull back; he was being too rough. Then he heard her little throaty moan, tasted it in his mouth.

He knew that sound. Imogen losing control. Imogen turning to flame and rapture in his arms. Imogen abandoned and eager.

Thierry's anger drained and with it the fear he'd refused to acknowledge. Fear that he'd lost her. Energy coursed through him; arousal weighted his groin and turned his body from flesh and bone to forged metal.

In a single, unhesitating movement, he swept an arm beneath her legs and scooped her up against his chest. Still they kissed, their lips fused with a passion that obliterated all else.

Her arms crept higher till he felt her fingers against his neck, holding tight. He wanted to whoop in exultation. Except that would mean lifting his mouth from hers. And the way she was kissing him, as if she'd been starved of him, just as he'd been without her... He refused to give that up.

Thierry spun round, lifting his eyes just enough to navigate into Imogen's bedroom.

Six strides and he was beside the bed. An instant later

and she fell onto the coverlet, and he with her, arms around her, his body pressing her down. She hitched her arms tighter around his neck and pressed her mouth urgently against his.

With one hand he wrenched back the towel from her damp body, his fingers brushing soft flesh and dissolving his brain. Urgently, he fumbled at his belt buckle. He couldn't recall ever being this desperate, this uncoordinated.

He breathed hard through his nostrils, trying to find focus. He would have lifted his mouth but Imogen gripped his skull so hard he succumbed to mutual hunger and contented himself with fumbling one-handed.

One slim, bare leg slid alongside his, then folded over the back of his thigh, as if trapping him against her.

Did she really fear he'd withdraw now?

Not with the taste of her on his tongue, vanilla sugar and feminine spice. Not with her mouth demanding, playing, teasing his. And her body moving sinuously beneath him. Those tiny, circling movements drove him insane. He had to get naked, quickly, before he lost it.

He'd lost count of the weeks since he'd had Imogen. It felt like half a lifetime. The need for her rose, eclipsing all else. Finally, he wrenched his belt undone, then the button on his trousers. But in the process the back of his hand brushed the soft, warm skin of her belly.

A shaft of awareness struck him. Not sexual awareness but something new. Something powerful and tender. Bracing himself better on his other elbow, he turned his hand and spread his palm over her stomach.

There was a roaring in his ears, a pounding like a hundred horses behind his ribcage, and a strange new sense filling it. It was wonder, possessiveness and a fierce tug of protectiveness all rolled into one.

Imogen's head fell back and suddenly he could breathe again, though in rasping breaths so harsh they tore at his lungs. Or maybe that was because of the look in her eyes. It was something like wonderment and it erased his searing temper in an instant.

Thierry slid his hand lower, entranced by the incredible silky texture of her flesh and the fact that his child lay nestled there.

He wanted to pound himself against her, fill her hard and fast till they lost their minds in ecstasy. But thought of the child gave him pause. Exultation warred with caution—the primitive against the civilised.

'Our baby,' he murmured, stunned by the reality of it.

Imogen's hand covered his, gently pressing. Her eyes glowed as if he'd just given her the best compliment in the world.

'I thought you didn't really want it.'

He shook his head. In truth he hadn't thought too much about it as a living, breathing child. He'd focused on getting through the pregnancy, seeing Imogen cared for. Intellectually, he'd understood there was a baby, but touching her belly, knowing that new life lay just centimetres below his palm… It was a humbling experience.

He shook his head. 'I would never reject it.' That, at least, was the truth.

Imogen lay panting, watching expressions flicker across Thierry's strong features. He'd taken her from zero to two hundred in a heartbeat with that glorious, savage kiss that had melted her bones. Now his tenderness threatened to melt her heart.

Our baby. Finally, he'd said it. More than said it. He felt how special this was—it was there in his touch, his stillness, his expression.

Suddenly, he was moving and Imogen bit back a cry as he levered himself away. She had to clench her hands to stop herself reaching for him.

But he didn't go far, just pulling back far enough to strip

the towel wide, leaving her completely exposed. He bent, his mouth grazing her belly softly in a caress that drew her skin tight with wanting and wonder.

Imogen looked down at his glossy dark hair against her skin, that proud face, his large, capable hand clamping her hip while his lips skated across the place where their baby lay.

Her heart turned over at Thierry's tenderness, and stupidly, tears pricked the back of her eyes. Rapidly, she blinked them back.

'You really do care about the baby.' The revelation tightened her throat.

His eyes met hers and connection throbbed between them, strong as the beat of her heart. 'Of course I care.'

Imogen shook her head, confused by what she thought she saw in his eyes. 'There's no need for this…us.' She stumbled over the words, hating the idea that, for the sake of their baby, he might pretend to want her too.

'No need?' His dark brows scrunched together.

She tried to hitch herself higher in the bed but his weight imprisoned her.

'You don't want me. There's no need to pretend.'

'Not *want* you?' His eyes rounded.

Imogen looked away, too aware suddenly of her nakedness. 'When I went to your room, when I wanted you, you rejected me.' Sheer pride kept her voice steady when it felt like she was crumbling into a thousand humiliated pieces.

'Listen to me, Imogen.' His hand was warm and compelling as he cupped her chin, turning it so she was forced to meet his gaze. 'I never, not even for a moment, stopped wanting you.'

'But—'

'But I tried to ignore that because I needed to look after you. I thought you were too sick, too fragile—'

'Fragile!' Her eyes bulged.

Thierry nodded. 'I was trying to protect you from me.'

Slowly the grim line of his mouth eased into a rakish smile that made her heart dance. 'But you're not ill now, are you?' His voice grazed her nerves like suede on silk.

Imogen opened her mouth to argue, to probe, but abruptly he was gone, sliding down her body. 'Thierry?'

He positioned himself low, his strong hands urging her thighs up and out, leaving her wide open to him. Imogen's breath stalled, her protest disintegrating as those midnight-dark eyes snared hers. His mouth dipped to touch her in that most sensitive spot and a shiver of powerful excitement shot through her. She'd waited so long for his loving. Wonder filled her at the idea he, like she, had suffered from the careful distance they'd maintained.

Imogen swallowed hard, but before she could formulate words his mouth caressed her again. This time the bolt of pleasure rocked her to the core.

Seconds later, her heart quivering from the smoky expression in his eyes, the flames erupted and her whole body lit up from the inside. The climax was more powerful than any Imogen remembered. She found herself sobbing his name, her hands biting his shoulders as waves of pleasure rolled through her.

Afterwards he didn't smile. There was no satisfaction like he'd shown in the past when she hadn't been able to contain her response to him. His expression was serious, completely intent as he gently lowered her legs, stroking her thighs till the racking shudders of ecstasy abated.

Through half-closed eyes she watched him undress, revealing the lean, powerful body that was so superbly masculine and honed to perfection. His movements were methodical and slow, as if he didn't understand how much she needed him, even after that climax. No, because of it. She needed Thierry, his body joined with hers.

Finally, he covered her with his hard frame, careful to take his weight on his arms. Heavy thighs pressed against hers, the rough silk dusting of his chest hair tickled her nipples and she sighed, relishing his heavy erection nudging her.

Imogen clutched his shoulders, trying to draw him closer, but he resisted, his jaw locked in an expression of determination that flummoxed her. But soon she understood.

It wasn't enough that he'd already reduced her to white-hot ash with that blast of sexual release. He was determined to do it again, with his superb body and his hand between her legs.

'I want you. Now,' she gasped, letting go of his shoulder and reaching for him. But she'd barely brushed her fingers across that hot erection when he captured both her wrists and shackled them above her head with one hand.

'Thierry!' But his mouth met hers, stopping her complaints, and all the while he made love to her with a slow, sure eroticism that made her tremble all over again. Heat sparked anew and she jerked hard beneath his touch as rapture took her.

How long he pleasured her she didn't know but she saw stars over and over again. Her breathing fractured and her body was limp and boneless from an overload of delight.

All the while those dark eyes held hers, his touch sure and fatally sensual, dragging response after response from her. Imogen told herself she should have stopped him, demanded what she wanted. But how could she when it seemed he knew her better than she did? He played her body like a maestro conducting a symphony. A symphony that left her euphoric and sated.

She felt as if those caresses had indelibly imprinted him on her body, marking her as his, so that in future she'd respond to no man but him. She was lost in the heady delight of his touch, his slow, seductive kisses and the magic he wove.

Finally, he came to her, joining them with one slow surge that brought him right to the heart of her. For an instant he held steady there and she wondered if she'd ever know again such a sensation of being one with another being. It was wonderful and scary and, despite her exhaustion, arousing.

Wrapping her arms around his slick torso, she held him close. He was determined to take things slowly, his movements measured, despite the way his heart pounded. Looking up, she saw the sheen of sweat on his forehead and the grit of a jaw locked, as if in pain. His heat was like a furnace, branding her.

A flash of suspicion hit. Was he afraid he'd injure the baby? Was that what kept his powerful body so tight?

As soon as the notion surfaced she knew it was true. He'd been mightily aroused from the moment he'd confronted her in the bathroom and still he held himself in check.

Her hands slid down the sleek curve of his back and around the impressive, taut curve of his buttocks. They flexed at her touch, and she tightened her grip, hearing Thierry's breath hiss. She turned her head, stretching higher to touch her lips to his ear. Then she whispered to him, confiding exactly what she wanted him to do to her.

She'd barely begun when he lost his slow rhythm and a burst of hoarse French filled her ears. A large hand clamped her breast, kneading, as Thierry's hips jerked powerfully, rocking into her, filling her faster and faster.

Imogen held tight, revelling in his urgency. She nipped at his earlobe and suddenly there was a roar of sound, a fierce, undulating wave of delight as he powered into her, no longer in control, as vulnerable to ecstasy as she'd been.

Heat pumped into her, an unfettered liquid throb that she'd never before experienced.

Dazedly, Imogen realised it was the first time they hadn't used protection. Maybe that was why this felt so momentous. So starkly real as she held Thierry's shuddering body protectively close. Not just satisfying, but as if together they'd discovered some primeval secret that would bind them for ever.

Finally, he slumped in her arms, his mouth at her neck, his weight pressing her down as exhaustion and satiation claimed them.

Imogen's last thought was a hope that, whatever they'd just experienced, it would change everything between them.

CHAPTER TEN

'ARE YOU HUNGRY?' The warm rumble of Thierry's voice made Imogen stir and stretch. She'd been lying in a haze of wellbeing, her mind drifting.

She opened her eyes and discovered soft lamplight filled the room. 'How long did I sleep?' She rolled over to find him propped against the headboard beside her. He looked scrumptious with his rumpled hair, the dark shadow on his jaw, and a casual shirt and jeans.

'You got dressed!'

His chuckle was like honey, rich and enticing, and her insides curled. Delight feathered her spine and between her thighs she felt a pulse flutter into life.

Responding again to the sensual promise in Thierry's voice should have been impossible after all they'd just shared. Yet when her eyes met his the impact of that connection jolted through her. She watched his smile fade.

'I had to get dressed or shock the staff when I went to get us a snack. You might prefer me naked but they wouldn't.'

Imogen wouldn't bet on it. No woman in her right mind would object to seeing a man like Thierry in all his glory—beautifully proportioned, every muscle honed and full of lean power. Watching him walk naked across a room was one of the treats she'd most missed when they'd said their goodbyes in Paris. He was built like an athlete in his prime, moving with effortless masculine grace.

'What time is it?' Surely it had been early afternoon when he'd confronted her in the bathroom? After her long walk in the sun, grappling with her options for the future, she'd felt weary and hot, ready for a cool shower.

He shrugged. 'Late. I cancelled dinner while you slept but Jeanne insisted I bring a tray to you.'

Imogen rose on her elbows. 'You should have woken me.'

Thierry didn't answer. His gaze was on her breasts, uncovered now by the sheet that someone had pulled over her. Heat suffused Imogen. Because she was so exhausted by their love-making she didn't even remember covering herself? Or because of the jangle of excitement when he looked at her that way—as if she were some delicacy for his enjoyment? She was so weak where he was concerned. Look how she'd gone up in flames in his arms!

Imogen grabbed the sheet and pulled it higher.

'Don't.' His arm shot out, fingers circling her wrist. 'Please.' His deep voice grated.

She swallowed, a delicate shiver rippling through her as he let go her wrist to touch her breast with gentle fingers. Was it his touch or the pleading tone that made her hesitate?

A gasp caught in her throat as pleasure cascaded through her. Her nipple beaded to an aching pout as he circled her breast.

'Thierry.' It was half groan, half plea, and she didn't have time to feel self-conscious about it because in another second he was there, his breath warm on her flesh, his eyes glittering greedily.

One arm pulled her close while the other cupped her breast as he lowered his mouth. Her skin tingled as he blew over her nipple, creating delicious quivers of reaction that spread across her back, down her belly and straight to her womb. Then his mouth was on her, drawing her in, offering bone-melting delight.

Imogen cradled his dark head in her hands, holding him to her while her hips turned towards him, pressing close through the bedclothes. She loved the softness of his hair in her hands, such a contrast to the hard muscle and bone of his powerful body.

When finally he dragged his head up her breathing was ragged and needy and she had trouble focusing on his expression.

'I came here to talk,' he murmured. 'But that can wait.' Already, he was peeling the sheet lower, his big, warm hand smoothing down her ribs.

She covered his fingers with hers, stopping his progress. 'You want to talk?'

'Later will do.' A hungry smile curled the corner of Thierry's mouth, and Imogen knew a compelling temptation simply to lie back and enjoy his attentions. Nothing in all her life made her feel so good as when he made love to her.

Except ever since the doctor's news, she'd wanted to talk with Thierry. Not the casual chatter that he'd used to fill her 'celebration' lunch, but to sort out things between them.

Lustrous dark eyes surveyed her. Oh, the promise in that heated look! 'It can wait.'

How she'd craved that from him all this time when he'd been punctiliously polite, like a courteous stranger.

Nerves stabbed her. He'd said he still desired her, had already proved it, yet maybe she wouldn't like what he'd say. They needed to clear the air and decide where they went from here. It took all her courage to do what she knew she must.

'No, it can't.' She put her hand on his shoulder, stopping him when he would have bent again to her breast. She felt the bunch and flex of muscle beneath her hand and knew she didn't have the power to hold him off. Instead, he chose to respect her wishes.

Finally, she felt some of his urgency abate a fraction as he eased back, resignation on his face. 'You choose the damnedest times to chat.'

A bubble of laughter rose to her lips but she smothered it, realising it was generated by nerves, not amusement. 'You were the one who suggested we talk.'

'That was before.' He moved his hand to tweak her nipple. She gasped as a chord of erotic energy drew tight and alive to the core of her being. Slowly, Thierry smiled. 'Are you sure you don't want to talk later?'

Of course she wasn't sure. She was only human.

Too human when it came to Thierry. For a woman who had no trouble resisting men, she found herself totally unstuck with this gorgeous hunk of a Frenchman. Even the lazy satisfaction of her well-used body didn't prevent a quiver of anticipation at the look in his eyes.

'We need to talk now.' Her voice, throaty and full, gave her away but finally, after close scrutiny, he nodded and rolled away from her to sit up.

Imogen gnawed at her lip rather than howl her frustration at the distance between them.

This is what you wanted, remember!

Physically, she was besotted with the man. She yanked up the sheet, determined to cover herself, and almost groaned out loud at the sensual torture of crisp cotton against her aroused nipples.

Out of the corner of her eye she saw him watching. Was that a smirk?

Did he know how turned on she was after the way he'd fondled her? Of course he knew! He was enjoying her reaction.

Setting her mouth, Imogen let go of the sheet and wriggled up into a sitting position, propping a second pillow behind her. Warm air caressed her breasts but it was the heat of Thierry's gaze that she felt like a touch.

He wasn't smiling now. He was focused on every sway and jiggle of her bare breasts with an intensity that almost stopped her breath.

Good! Served him right.

Casually, she reached for the sheet, drawing it slowly over her chest and tucking it tight under her arms.

She turned to him. 'You're ready to talk?'

'Witch.' But there was amusement in his eyes despite the tension in his features.

If she was, then it was because of him. Thierry Girard had turned a cautious mouse of a woman into one more than happy to flaunt herself before her lover. One with more confidence in her body than she'd had before. One ready to take on the challenge of living instead of dying.

Imogen felt an answering smile tug her mouth. She loved it when he was like this—charming, fun and oh-so-sexy. Far better than when he'd been politely distant. Or when he'd looked grim and implacable.

'Thierry? We've got things to discuss.'

Slowly, he raised his gaze to hers and once more she felt that sensation of melding, of connection. It warmed her in places that had been too long cold.

'Let's eat first.' He swung away and lifted a tray from the bedside table, busying himself ensuring it was stable.

In any other man those quick, restless movements would have made her wonder if he was nervous.

But this was Thierry, über-confident and competent, literally the lord of all he surveyed from his ancient *château*. What reason could he have to be nervous?

She was the outsider, the unwanted complication in his world.

Thick, dark hair fell across his brow, giving him a casual, boyish look that tugged at her heart.

Imogen's breath caught as she remembered his grandmother's words. Did she really look at him with love in her eyes? Was that why she was so desperate for more than his polite goodwill? Why she craved his smiles and this precious sense of them sharing not just their bodies, but some other intimate connection?

The idea made her simultaneously ecstatic and horrified. Trepidation and tentative hope danced along her nerves. But she couldn't bring herself to believe it was true. It was far too dangerous a thought.

'Fruit, quiche or trout?'

Imogen made herself focus on the lavish spread between them. Jeanne had done them proud. She could barely see the tray for the luscious food piled upon it.

Suddenly she realised she was ravenous. 'Everything.' She plucked a gleaming strawberry from a bowl. Her eyes closed as she bit into it. It tasted of sunlight and sweetness. She'd never known food to taste as good as here at Thierry's *château*. Because it was locally grown and fresh, or because her new lease of life made her appreciate small delights even more?

When she opened her eyes it was to find Thierry staring at her mouth, his expression taut and hungry. She gulped down the rest of the fruit, her throat constricting.

They had so much to sort out, but at least on a purely physical level the connection was as strong as ever. The intensity of Thierry's love-making earlier had given her hope and relief after these lonely days when he'd been away. Ever since her doctor's appointment she'd felt strangely alone, even when he was with her. He'd withdrawn mentally.

Not even the fact her headaches were fading had made her feel better. The last one, the first night Thierry had been away climbing, had been a mere shadow of the previous piercing agony.

'You're sure you want to talk?' His voice was pure temptation and the look in his eyes told her she'd enjoy every moment of *not* talking. But they needed to clear the air.

'Why were you so angry earlier?' Imogen had never seen him in a temper and riding that lashing storm had been shocking. Yet on some level she'd thrilled to the vibrancy in him, excited by it.

Because he cared enough to be angry?

That sounded masochistic and she wasn't fool enough to want a man who took out his frustrations on her. Yet she sensed Thierry's anger was rare. After all, he'd taken in his stride all the complications she'd presented him with, never once blaming her or losing his cool. It was more that his flash of temper had broken down the wall between them, the wall she hadn't seen him build till it was too late.

'I apologise for that.' A pulse ticked in his jaw as he helped himself to cheese and home-made crackers. 'I over-reacted. I see now you were trying to make a point.' Suddenly, he looked up, his eyes, dark as bitter coffee, snaring hers. 'But there was no need to prove yourself.'

Imogen spread her hands. 'It was important to make it clear I didn't want any more from you. You've done so much, acted so…honourably.' That old-fashioned word seemed apt. For surely that was what Thierry's grave concern, his gentleness and the efforts he'd gone to on her behalf, amounted to?

'It's done now. I suggest we forget it.' Yet he hadn't. There was an edge to his voice.

'But there's something bothering you.'

He dropped his gaze to her breasts, and her nipples peaked against the crisp cotton. 'From here everything looks perfect.'

Heat crept from her breasts to her throat and face. She still hadn't grown used to such blatantly carnal looks. They threatened to turn her brain as well as her bones to mush. After all, she'd spent twenty-five years avoiding risk, playing safe.

Thierry and her—this connection between them—had been easier to cope with when she'd been able to write it off as a flare of passing attraction, a desperate fling of a dying woman. But she had a full life before her now. She had to come to grips with what was happening.

Her whole being lit up when he looked at her that way. Focusing was almost impossible.

'Why do I get the feeling you're changing the subject?'

Thierry blinked and for an instant she read tension in that powerful frame.

'Things have changed,' he said finally. 'You were right about that.'

Imogen's frustration levels rose when he didn't continue. If he wouldn't confront the elephant in the room, she would.

'I'm not dying. Which means we've saddled ourselves with marriage when we needn't have.' The words tasted bitter.

'Saddled?' His nostrils flared as if in distaste.

'Come on, Thierry. Don't tell me you wanted a permanent wife. Marriage made sense when I thought I was dying and it meant you could claim our baby. But now—'

'Now you want to back out of it?'

'It's not a matter of backing out. It's a matter of being sensible.' The thought of leaving him tore at something vital inside her. But she owed him. That knowledge threatened to shatter every certainty she'd once harboured.

All her life she'd been risk-averse, carefully building security for herself, keeping herself independent of any man, she realised. No wonder Scott had found it so easy to walk away from her, using the time she'd devoted to her mother as an excuse. Now it seemed her happiness was bound up with a man she'd met just months ago.

Yet she couldn't hold Thierry to this marriage, not unless they were both committed to it. 'You were kind to me when I most needed it. I don't want to repay you with a complication you never wanted.'

No matter how she yearned for him.

Sexual attraction alone was not a sound basis for a relationship. As far as she knew, that was all he felt for her, plus responsibility for their baby.

'You think of our child as a complication?'

She struggled to read his inflection.

'It was unexpected, but I can't regret it. I was referring to me being a complication in your life.' Why was he so obtuse? His quick understanding was one of the things she loved about him.

Loved.

Something clenched in the deepest recesses of her soul.

It was true. It was really true.

Here she was, trying to convince him he didn't need a spouse, when all the time…

Imogen sucked in a deep breath, dizzy with the implications of the one crucial fact she'd been avoiding for weeks.

'Imogen?' Thierry's frown grew, lines ploughing his forehead and carving around his mouth.

Helplessly, she stared at him. She was in far too deep when the sight of his concern threatened to undo her resolve. She tried to tell herself that it was natural she'd grown fond of him when he'd been so wonderful.

But *fond* didn't go anywhere near describing her visceral need for Thierry. A need that was far more than physical.

Imogen crossed her arms as if to hide the tumultuous throb of her heart hurling itself against her ribs.

'I could be on a flight in a day or two.' She dragged the words out. 'There's no need for…' She waved her hand across the bed as words dissolved.

'You *want* to leave?' He leaned close, his finger stroking her cheek, pushing her hair back over her shoulder. It was all she could do not to turn into his touch and nestle her cheek against his palm.

She wanted so much. Thierry. This closeness. His passion—definitely his passion—but far more. She swallowed hard over a knot of pain.

Against the odds she'd shared a wonderful affair with a man who in every way the world counted was far out of her league. Now, when it should be over and they should be saying their goodbyes, it tore her apart.

Because it was true.

She'd fallen in love with Thierry Girard.

She wanted to be with him, not just now, sharing pleasure, but always, growing old together. Being a part of him just as he'd become a vital part of her.

'I'm trying to do what's right.' And it had never been so hard. To her horror her mouth crumpled with the effort of holding in so much welling emotion.

'I don't want you to go.' The words circled the still air and eddied deep inside her. Her head shot up, eyes locking with his.

'You don't?'

His smile was crooked and devastatingly sexy. 'I want you here, *chérie*.'

Imogen's heart locked in her throat. Could it be?

'Is it so bad being here with me?' he murmured, his hand trailing down her throat to her bare collarbone.

'Of course not. I…' She swallowed hard, trying to find her voice. 'I like it here.'

She'd like anywhere so long as Thierry was with her. The enormity of her feelings blindsided her. How had she gone from casual attraction to full-blown love in such a short space of time? Maybe because she wasn't made for casual affairs. That was why she'd been so cautious with her heart and her body before this.

'I'm glad. I'd wondered if it might be too quiet for you here.'

Imogen shook her head. She loved the peace of the estate. Besides, it was only minutes to the nearest town and a short drive to the nearest city. But what made it perfect was Thierry's presence.

'You really want me to stay?' Did he hear the longing in her voice? Hurriedly, she went on briskly. 'I'd rather you were totally honest.'

Thierry hesitated and there was something in his eyes that made her uneasy. As if he hid something.

Yet what could he hide? He had been trustworthy, honest and generous from the night they'd met. He'd even pulled back from her physically when he'd believed her ill, putting her wellbeing before his own sexual needs.

He wouldn't lie to her.

'I want you to stay, Imogen.' His gaze bored into hers, and she felt the impact right to her core. Slowly, he smiled and it was as if he'd flicked a switch, releasing the tension straining between them.

'Think about what we've got.' His hand dropped to the sheet covering her, his long fingers brushing her breasts in deliberate provocation. 'We like each other. We're sexually more than compatible.' He lifted his hand away and it was only then Imogen discovered how far she'd leaned forward into his touch. 'And we're having a child. Why not stay together?'

Dazed as much by his touch as his words, Imogen sank back against the pillows, her body heavy and lax.

'You want to stay married?' She needed to hear him spell it out.

'I do.' That smile devastated her brain, making logic almost impossible. 'It makes sense, Imogen.'

Part of her wanted to exult. He wanted her here, and not just as a temporary girlfriend. Imogen knew that a future with Thierry would be everything she'd never dared to hope for. Because when she was with him she felt…

'What we have is good, isn't it?'

Good?

Imogen's thoughts screeched to a halt.

Good. That insipid word couldn't describe how she felt when she was with Thierry.

She opened her mouth then closed it. Her neck prickled, the hairs standing to attention as finally her sluggish brain moved into gear.

She'd been on tenterhooks, wondering if he wanted her gone, but it was only now she realised what was missing.

Imogen met those gleaming eyes that she'd seen kindle with desire, crinkle with laughter or warm with concern. She took in those straight shoulders that she'd leaned on in moments of weakness and those capable hands that had helped her when she'd needed it. Thierry was caring, passionate and considerate.

But he doesn't love you.

There was no urgency in him, no desperation. Just calm logic and, yes, liking.

Imogen's heart skated to a bruising halt then lurched into a discordant rhythm so powerful she felt queasy.

Now she understood!

'This is you making the best of the situation, isn't it? Making do.' She recalled him talking in those terms in Paris, about not pining for the impossible, but adapting to whatever situation he found himself in.

'Why not?' That insouciant Gallic shrug made a mockery of her secret hopes and dreams. 'I'm expected to marry some time and here we are with a baby on the way.'

He must have noticed her breathless rigidity because he went on with a smile guaranteed to turn any woman to a puddle of pure longing. 'We like each other.' His hand settled on one of hers, lightly stroking an intricate scroll of desire from her wrist to her thumb. 'Sex between us is fantastic and we respect each other.'

'You said that before.' Her voice sounded scratchy. Were those the only reasons he could come up with for them to stay together?

'They're important.' The skin between his eyebrows pinched, as if he was surprised or annoyed she wasn't gushing with delight. 'I couldn't marry a woman I didn't respect.' His mouth curved in a way that devastated her resolve. 'As for the sex…' He shook his head. 'I can't remember it ever being so good.'

Imogen sat utterly still, scared that if she moved something, like her stupid heart, might shatter.

He wants to stay married to you because the sex is good. And because you're conveniently providing him with a child.

No doubt he wants one to inherit the estate and the villa

on the south coast, and all the other things the Girard family have amassed. He wants an heir.

She'd been dreaming of love but Thierry laid out their relationship as if it was a business merger.

Her lips flattened. That was how he saw this—a neat solution to a difficult problem. A way of keeping his child while getting companionship and sex into the bargain.

She had no illusions she was the sort of woman he'd marry in normal circumstances, but Thierry had proved himself a realist through and through. Why yearn for caviar when you have fish and chips already on the table?

Imogen felt her hair slide around her face and neck as she shook her head. 'I don't think that's a good basis for marriage.'

His hand tightened, long fingers shackling her wrist. Did he feel her pulse hammering? He leaned in, crowding her against the pillows. For the first time since this conversation began she felt disadvantaged, naked beneath the sheet while he was dressed.

'Of course it's a good basis for marriage.' His eyes narrowed. Fervently she hoped he couldn't read her thoughts. 'Unless you're after some fantasy of romance. Is that it?'

Self-preservation made her shake her head, even as her soul cried out that that was exactly what she wanted.

'I didn't think so.' His lips quirked up in the hint of a smile. 'You're like me, *chérie*—too practical to want hearts and flowers and sentimental protestations of undying love.'

Dry-eyed, Imogen gritted her teeth. Thierry couldn't know how she felt about him. He'd never deliberately trample over her feelings. Yet that didn't stop the pain from each dismissive word.

'You don't believe in love?'

His lips quirked. 'Once. I fell in love with a girl from a neighbouring estate. But she married someone else. At the time I thought my heart was broken but I'm old enough now to realise that's just a fiction. I've been happy with my life. It wasn't blighted by rejection after all.'

His expression was reflective as he stroked her palm, making her shiver. 'What we have is precious, Imogen, even if it doesn't go by the name of love. Respect, liking and a baby—those make a good starting point.'

'Don't forget the sex,' she said, hiding pain behind a twisted smile.

'Oh, I don't. Not for a moment.' He pressed his mouth to the spot below her ear where she was most sensitive. Instantly, tremors of heat racked her, and she shivered. Yet her heart ached.

'Let me warm you properly, Imogen.' He reached for the tray between them, made to lift it away, but she put a shaky hand on his arm.

'No. Don't. I'm hungry.' The food would be sawdust in her mouth but she couldn't have sex with him, not now. Not knowing she'd given her heart to him and he only saw her as a convenient solution to a problematic situation.

She didn't care about his wealth or his power. But she wanted to *matter* to someone, to be the most important thing in their life. And that someone was Thierry. Because that was how she felt about him. Once she'd have settled but now she didn't want to *make do*. She wanted *everything*.

But he didn't believe in love. Would he ever? If he did, would it be for her or some woman from his own set, privileged and sophisticated?

Bile rose, and she almost choked.

'Are you all right?' The concern in his eyes was real.

Thierry did care. Just not enough.

'Fine,' she croaked, reaching for the sparkling water on the tray. She had to hold the glass in both hands so as not to spill it, but at least that gave her something to concentrate on other than Thierry's piercing gaze.

She felt his scrutiny like a touch. He wanted an answer.

What was she going to do? Flounce home and give up

any chance he might, over time, begin to care for her as she did him? Or stay here like some charity case, making do with what he handed out, maybe breaking her heart little by little each day?

The mineral water tasted unbearably metallic, and she put it down with a grimace.

'Maybe I won't have anything to eat after all.'

'You're unwell? Morning sickness?' Thierry whipped away the tray, getting off the bed to put it on a nearby table. Imogen's breath eased out in a sigh of relief. She needed space to think.

'I'm a little out of sorts.' After one swift glance at his frown she looked away, watching her hands smooth the rumpled sheet. How had she gone from ecstasy to misery in such a short space of time?

It wasn't as if he'd led her on. He'd been marvellous. It was all her own doing, because she'd made the mistake of believing the fantasy. Because she loved him.

'I'll get you some herbal tea.'

'No. Nothing, thanks.' She doubted she'd keep anything down.

'Lie down then and I'll stay here till you sleep.'

'No!' Her head shot around to find him staring at her curiously. 'No, there's no need.'

See? He was caring. The sort of man any woman would want, even if he didn't love her. Was she crazy to wish for more?

She must be. Why would a man born to his world of privilege and power fall for someone as ordinary as her?

A warm hand closed around hers. He stood beside the bed, so close she had to crick her neck to meet his eyes. They were unfathomable, deep and steady, yet she felt the intensity of his stare through every part of her being.

'So you'll stay, Imogen? You agree?'

She imagined tension in his voice. Clearly, she was projecting her own emotions.

'I...'

'You won't regret it. We're good together; you know it.'

Good. There was that word again.

She didn't want good. She wanted spectacular, amazing, special. She wanted love.

She gnawed at her lip, torn between fighting for what she wanted and the craven impulse to take whatever Thierry offered. She wasn't sure she'd like the woman she'd become if she did that.

'Stay, Imogen.' His voice was compelling, his hold tight.

She swallowed hard. 'I'll stay. For now. Let's see how it goes.'

CHAPTER ELEVEN

SEE HOW IT GOES.

She was going to see how it went.

As if he were on probation!

Thierry frowned, flipping another page of the contract before realising he hadn't taken in a word.

Disgusted, he shoved his chair back from the desk.

His ability to concentrate, even in a crisis, had always been one of his strengths. It had saved his hide more than once on long-distance motor rallies and while climbing. It had been one of the few assets he'd had in the early days when he took on this business.

Until today concentrating on what needed to be done hadn't been a problem. Even when he'd yearned for the wind in his hair and a far more physical challenge than that presented by corporate negotiations. He'd always given his all to the job at hand, knowing the sooner he solved a problem and moved on, the sooner he'd be free.

Nowadays he even found satisfaction in developing and expanding the business, finding new opportunities.

Not today.

A month today since Imogen had agreed to stay and *see how it goes.*

A month and no resolution.

He felt like he was on trial.

He surged to his feet and stalked to the window, staring at the blue sky that mocked his mood. He felt dark, stormy and miserable.

Thierry folded his arms over his chest. Made miserable by a woman. It didn't seem possible. Never had it happened in all the years since Sandrine had rejected him and his volatile young heart had counted itself broken.

Since then he'd enjoyed women but never wanted or expected anything serious.

Naturally, that had changed with Imogen. She was his wife so they needed a secure, meaningful relationship. One based on respect.

That was what he'd offered her and still she refused to commit to staying.

What more could she want?

He spun around, his gaze driving unerringly through the office's glass wall to his cousin Henri's desk. There he was, his head bent towards Imogen's.

Heat blasted Thierry's gut as he watched the pair, so at ease, totally absorbed in the accounts Thierry personally found incredibly dull. But Imogen and Henri spoke the same language. The language of numbers.

When Imogen had complained she didn't have enough to keep her busy—as if she needed to work when he could provide for her!—Thierry had suggested she assist with the accounts. It had been a masterstroke and a disaster. Imogen was happy with the opportunity to work as an accountant again, her smiles becoming more genuine and frequent, at least in the office. More than that, she'd proved a valuable asset, her skills obviously top notch.

But her happiness at work only made him realise how rarely she smiled with him. He missed those lit-from-within smiles, so incandescent they were contagious.

His eyes narrowed as he heard a laugh and watched Imogen and Henri share some joke.

Thierry wanted to stride out and yank her away. Insist she share the joke with him as once she would have.

Except it didn't work like that. With him she was polite, friendly, as she was with Jeanne or his grandparents when they visited. But never was he treated to those delicious gurgles of pure joy that had entranced him when they'd met. Or those cheeky, teasing grins.

He missed that. Missed Imogen. It was as if the most vital part of her was locked somewhere he couldn't reach.

Sometimes when they made love he felt he'd almost breached that gap, reached the woman locked behind her reserve. For, despite initial protests, Imogen hadn't been able to deny the passion between them. They shared a bed and his one solace was that in his arms she went up in flames as surely as the propane that fuelled his balloon flights. She was mesmerising, her passion all he could ask for.

Yet afterwards a curious blankness replaced the smoky flare of rapture. She'd withdraw mentally. For the first time ever Thierry found himself wanting to dig deeper, even discuss her *feelings*!

She drove him crazy.

He wrapped a palm around the back of his neck. He was too close to the edge.

Thierry glared through the glass. *Diable.* He wasn't jealous of his cousin, was he?

Impossible. Yet he found himself striding across the office, only to slam to a halt, his hand on the door.

Think, man! What are you going to do? Go out and drag her off to your bedroom?

The idea appealed, especially when he saw her smile at Henri as the younger man touched her hand then pointed to something on the screen. Waves of heat battered at Thierry, turning his belly into a churning morass.

Okay, he admitted it. He was jealous. He knew there was nothing between them except liking and professional admiration but that didn't lessen his envy.

Thierry dropped the door handle as if it burned with an electric current. He took a step back.

What was happening to him?

He wasn't interested in examining his feelings. He

wanted action. But abducting his wife and ravishing her till she cried his name in rapture, while perfect in its own way, would leave him disgruntled when she withdrew again.

Sex wasn't the answer. Not alone. He had to find another way to connect with Imogen.

'Imogen.' She stilled, her heart pattering as that deep voice turned her name into a caress.

Would she ever *not* respond to it?

Slowly, she turned, willing her breathing to steady as espresso-dark eyes snared hers and she tingled all over. It was hard, sometimes, to remember Thierry saw her as a convenient wife, not the love of his life. That heavy-lidded stare sizzled with a promise she'd almost swear held more than physical desire.

Except she was done with fantasy. She was back into self-protection mode, carefully weighing her options for the future. She owed her baby that.

'Thierry.' She stumbled a little over his name. Last time she'd said it had been just hours ago, in that big, luxurious bed of his, and she hadn't said it: she'd screamed it in pleasure. 'Did you need this report? We're almost done.' Casually, she glanced at Henri, hoping he'd take up the conversation.

'It's not about the report,' Thierry said. 'I need you.'

Imogen's head snapped around. But the banked embers in his eyes had disappeared, or maybe she'd imagined that. Thierry looked all business.

'Of course. Excuse me, Henri?'

'Yes, fine.' He turned back to the spreadsheet. 'We've almost sorted this. You'll have it in ten minutes, Thierry.'

'No rush. So long as I get it by this evening.'

Imogen frowned. An hour ago the report had been urgent. But her thoughts frayed when Thierry put a hand under her elbow as she stood.

Once she'd loved those little courtesies. Now they were exquisite torture.

'You want me for something?' Her voice was only a little husky.

'I do.' To her surprise, he escorted her out to the car park where the sun shone warm on her face. 'I suppose I'll need to get another car,' he murmured as they approached his.

'You will?' The words flummoxed her. He adored his low-slung sports car.

'There's no room for a baby seat in this.'

The idea of Thierry replacing his streamlined beast with a family sedan stunned her. He really was serious about being an involved father.

If she stayed.

'Why are we here?' She stood back when he opened the passenger door. 'I've got work to do.'

'You've done your share today.'

Imogen shook her head. 'It's early—'

'You married the boss, so there are perks. Besides…' his expression turned serious '…you need to look after yourself. You're still getting morning sickness.'

'Only a little.' She found it better if she kept herself busy. Between the accountancy work, intensive French lessons and the hours she spent with Jeanne learning the secrets of French baking, every waking hour was filled. Soon she'd have to decide whether to leave, but having time on her hands hadn't helped her reach a decision. All it had done was depress her.

'Well, today we have somewhere else to be.' He held open the door. Imogen wavered, for suddenly it hit her—she'd deliberately arranged her days to spend as little time as possible with her husband.

Because she was afraid he'd convince her to stay?

'Please, Imogen. It's important.' His mouth flattened. Curiously, she read strain in his proud features and restlessness in the way his hand slid along the open door.

'What's wrong?' Anxiety leapt into her chest. She'd learned no one was immune to bad news and she'd never seen Thierry look this way, as if suppressing agitation.

'Nothing's wrong. Can't you just trust me?'

Imogen looked into the face of the man she loved and knew that was the one thing she'd always done. He'd never deliberately hurt her. He'd gone to remarkable lengths to protect her.

She laid her hand on his where it shifted along the door. Instantly, he stilled, and she felt the familiar thrill of connection. 'Of course I trust you.' Whatever Thierry wanted, she'd help him if she could. She owed him that.

Yet she was careful not to meet that gleaming gaze as she slid into the passenger seat.

'I can't believe it. This is amazing!' The wind caught her words as hair streamed across her face. Imogen laughed, lifting her free hand to pull her hair back.

The air rushed around her, skimming her body just as the small sailing boat skimmed the lake's sparkling waters. The sensation of speed, the huff and ripple of the wind against canvas and the joyous sense of adventure were like champagne in her blood. Her skin tingled, and her heart felt lighter than it had in months.

Thierry beamed, his face creasing into grooves that accentuated his devastating appeal. He looked totally at ease, his long frame swaying, adjusting easily each time the small boat shifted. Yet she'd seen how quickly he could move, coming to her aid whenever an unexpected change in conditions threatened her fragile confidence. She was a complete novice.

But he'd made sailing so easy.

Her hand clenched on the tiller. That was what he'd always done, wasn't it? Make things easy for her. Their affair. Their baby. Even dying. No matter what she'd faced, he'd been at her side.

Her heart lurched against her ribs. She loved him so much. How was she supposed to walk away? Was she mad, even considering it?

'I knew you'd take to it.' He linked his arms behind his head, stretching those long legs towards her till they almost touched.

'You couldn't possibly know that.'

'Of course I did. Face it, Imogen, we're the same. Both with a taste for adventure.'

Automatically, she shook her head. She wasn't like Thierry. Those extreme sports he enjoyed made her hair curl. 'You've got me wrong, Thierry. I'm ordinary and cautious. I'm an accountant, remember? Until recently I'd never done anything exciting. Only the threat of dying got me out of Australia.'

'But it did, didn't it? You didn't stay, waiting for the end, but went out and found your true self.' He sounded satisfied, almost smug, as if today's surprise sailing treat was a major win in some way she couldn't fathom.

'I'm afraid not.' How could he have got her so wrong? 'My true self belongs at home or in an office. This is just…' She shrugged. 'My sister was the courageous one, not me.'

The wind shifted and the little boat shivered as Imogen struggled to guide it. Instantly, Thierry was beside her, his shoulder against hers, his hand over hers on the tiller. Seconds later they were gliding easily over the water again. He lifted his hand but didn't move away.

A sense of wellbeing filled her, and for once Imogen didn't fight it, just accepted this glorious moment, with the rush of wind, the thrill of sailing and Thierry beside her.

'You don't think it took courage to look after your dying mother? Even though it cost you your lover? You don't think you were courageous when you faced what you thought was your own death? Or when you planned to face pregnancy alone?'

'I didn't have any choice. That wasn't courage. That was necessity.'

Thierry lifted her free hand to his lips and her heart sang. 'You're wrong, Imogen. You're exciting and marvellous and brave. We're well matched—because we both have a taste for *life*.'

She opened her mouth to disagree but his finger on her lips stopped her. 'We *are*, Imogen. Don't you feel it whenever we're together?'

The trouble was she did. But she told herself it was because she'd fallen for him, hook, line and sinker. Whereas he— Well, Thierry wouldn't fall for someone like her.

'You're talking to a woman who has just spent days learning how to make the perfect choux pastry. I'm no daredevil.'

Thierry shook his head. 'You think it's so black and white? That we aren't all complex? I might love motor rallies and alpine climbing but I never spent all my time doing that. Do you know how many hours I spent beneath the engine of my rally car, getting it tuned to perfection? Or planning the optimal route for a trek?' He slipped his arm around her, his embrace warming her in places she couldn't name.

'You don't understand. I'm not the woman you think I am. That woman in Paris wasn't the real Imogen.'

'Wasn't she?' His voice was a deep burr that did wicked things to her heart and her self-control. 'You've spent so long putting yourself in a pigeonhole you can't see that you're more complex than you ever imagined.' He paused. 'I think that's why you're afraid to take a chance on me.'

Before she could say anything he rose and took up a position just far enough away that she couldn't touch him. But his eyes held hers, bright and challenging.

'We have so much going for us, Imogen. Why won't you give us a chance? Us and our child?'

Because I'm scared. I'm terrified to love you when you don't love me back.

'Trust your instincts, Imogen. Think of the good times we could have together.' His was the voice of temptation, coursing through her like liquid chocolate.

Of course she wanted to stay. That was the trouble. It was too easy to imagine being with him, spending time together, not just at the *château* or in his arms, but *living*, sharing adventures like this.

'All you have to do is let go of your fear and trust in us.'

Let go of her fear! After living with fear so long that was easier said than done. Yet the temptation to trust in him was almost overwhelming. Only a lifetime's caution held her back.

But what was she holding back from? Fear of not being loved? If she walked away from Thierry she'd sever whatever bond they already had. Plus she'd destroy any chance that he'd ever love her.

Did she ask too much, expecting him to love after such a short time, just because she loved him? Imogen frowned. Looked at that way, she seemed impatient and greedy.

Imogen stared at his sprawled body, apparently relaxed, yet with eyes so watchful. He'd deliberately distanced himself when it would be easy to persuade her with his arm around her. Her mind always went to mush when he touched her.

He was being noble, damn him, and to her chagrin that only made it harder to deny him. But he wouldn't be the man she adored if he wasn't decent and caring. Look at today—giving her this first exhilarating taste of sailing.

Her thoughts stuck and circled. Thierry had shared his love of the outdoors with her, his delight in speed and adventure.

He wasn't blocking her out of his life, or taking her for granted like the convenient bride she'd imagined herself.

He was letting her in.

Imogen stared hard at the man before her, the tautness of his shoulders and hands revealing he was anything but relaxed. He wasn't cold-blooded. He might see marriage as a pragmatic solution to their situation but Thierry was passionate and caring. He didn't love her but surely there was a chance he might one day?

If she stayed.

Her heart pounded like stampeding wild animals and she blinked, blinded by the sudden brightness of sunshine on glittering water.

'Watch out!' A moment later he was with her again, his firm body hot beside her, his strong hand guiding hers.

The boat shifted, poised for a moment, then turned and caught the wind, flying across the water.

But it wasn't the speed that caught the breath in Imogen's throat.

She sank against him, her head against his chest, his tantalising scent stimulating her senses. She closed her eyes and felt the tension leave her.

Really, she had only one choice.

'You win, Thierry. I'll stay.'

It might be the biggest gamble of her life, the only gamble, but she'd play it to the end.

CHAPTER TWELVE

THIERRY'S HANDS CAME around her waist, pulling her back against him. In the mirror she read that familiar smile, and her stomach tumbled over itself as it had that first night in Paris.

'You look good enough to eat.' He pressed a kiss to her neck, and she shivered as desire spiked.

'Seriously, this dress is right for tonight?' It was her first formal event as Thierry's hostess and nerves had struck. When he'd mentioned it a month ago she'd told herself wearing one of Izzy's creations would be perfect. The full-length white satin with crimson flowers would give her confidence. It was the dress she'd worn the night she'd met Thierry and it felt like a lucky talisman.

Should she have taken his offer to buy something new?

'This dress is perfect.' He spread his palm over her belly, now rounded just enough that she'd had to find a dress-maker to let out the dress a little.

'Even if I'm making it strain at the seams?' Surely she'd put on weight in the past week? Soon she'd need new bras too.

Thierry's hand slid up to her breasts straining against the satin. His light touch made her knees quiver. 'The only problem will be the disgruntled women when all men watch you, *ma chérie*.'

Imogen's lips twitched. 'Sweet talker.'

'Siren.' His hand stroked her budding nipple, and she gasped in exquisite arousal. Pregnancy made her even more sensitive to his touch. And he knew it. In the mirror his smile was pure erotic invitation as she sank back against him.

It had been so easy to give in and agree to live as Thierry's wife. He made her feel desired, appreciated, supported. Even if he didn't love her, surely that was enough to begin a marriage? And their sex life just got better and better. She read familiar heat in his expression.

'Thierry! We don't have time. And I've got my make-up on.'

Firmly, she stifled a wish that he felt more than sexual attraction. She needed patience. One day surely…?

He pressed an open-mouthed kiss to her neck that made her shiver, then stepped back. Instantly, she felt bereft. She was as needy as ever and now she'd opened her heart to him too.

'I'll be good. Besides, I have something for you.'

'You do?' She made to turn but he stopped her.

'Stand there.' She watched, dumbfounded, as he lowered a magnificent necklace over her head. The dressing-room light flashed on brilliant gems and old gold that glowed with the patina of age. Imogen was dazzled as the weight of the necklace settled on her.

'I've heard of rubies the size of pigeons' eggs…' she said shakily.

'You think it too old-fashioned?'

'It's gorgeous,' she murmured. 'I just hope it's not as precious as it looks. Tell me it's costume jewellery.'

He shook his head. 'It's real. You're my wife, my hostess. You need to look the part. This has been in the family for generations. Besides, it matches your dress.'

He was right. The crimson glow of the central stone matched the flowers on her dress and the ornate necklace paired well with the simplicity of the strapless bodice.

Her fingers fluttered over it, her eyes wide. She looked different—not like the woman she knew.

Disquiet shivered through her, but she forced it aside. Naturally Thierry wanted her to do him proud tonight. The session he'd organised for her with a beautician had been a thoughtful gift. Thierry's grandmother had spent hours coaching her on the who's who of French society that would be at tonight's party. Plus, with her language tutor's help, Imogen felt reasonably competent with introductions and very basic conversation.

She smoothed her gloved hands down her dress, telling herself she'd be fine. It wasn't that she was scared of crowds, just that they weren't her thing. But with Thierry at her side she'd be fine. More than fine. She'd shine.

Only Thierry didn't stay at her side.

For an hour he was with her, his arm around her waist, greeting their guests, turning these sophisticated strangers into people she could relax and laugh with. Most of them, if curious about her, were friendly.

But after a while they got separated. Occasionally he'd turn his head to check on her, his eyebrows raised in question, and she'd nod, silently letting him know she was okay.

She was a professional woman, used to meeting strangers. She didn't need her hand held, even if some of the glitterati were rather daunting.

There was one woman in particular—Sandrine. A tall, slender blonde who looked like she'd stepped from a glossy magazine. She was the most beautiful woman Imogen had ever seen, with a long sweep of platinum hair, perfect features and an assurance that allowed her to wear backless silver lamé and a fortune in diamonds with casual insouciance.

But it wasn't the other woman's beauty that made Imogen stare, it was the realisation that this was the woman who'd broken Thierry's heart. Sandrine made it clear they'd known each other since the cradle. Several times in their short conversation she'd subtly reinforced the fact that Imogen was an outsider in this milieu.

When Thierry was beside Imogen that didn't matter. But as the evening wore on it was harder not to make comparisons between herself and the glamorous blonde so at home in these superb surroundings.

Imogen dragged her attention back to the couple talking with her about Australia, reminiscing about a trip to an exclusive resort she'd heard of but never visited.

'I was disappointed,' the husband said, 'not to see those dangerous snakes we hear about.' The twinkle in his eyes belied the complaint.

Imogen smiled. 'I can recommend some nature reserves for your next visit.' She glanced down and noticed their glasses were empty. Looking around, she couldn't see any of the waiters brought in for tonight's party.

'If you'll excuse me, I'll send someone over with drinks.'

'No, no, it's fine. It's no trouble.'

Nice as it was to chat, it felt good to do something practical, attending to guests' needs. It made her feel less of an imposter in this well-heeled crowd. To be fair, though, not all the invitees were rich. There were locals and friends of Thierry who shared an interest in extreme sports.

Imogen was moving to the end of the room where the bar was set up when a woman's voice slowed her steps.

'Of course she's pregnant, what other reason could there be? He's married her to make the child legitimate. She's not Thierry's type. When has anyone ever seen him with a brunette? And as for the rest… Thierry deserves someone with panache, someone who fits in.'

Pale blonde hair swung across the speaker's elegant bare back.

Sandrine. Thierry's old friend. His first love.

Imogen's chest tightened and she faltered to a stop. Was that why Thierry was adamant he'd never want a love match? Because he'd given his heart to this woman and no one else would fill her place?

It was one thing to know her husband had once been disappointed in love. It was quite another to discover the object of his affection was the most stunningly beautiful woman she'd ever seen.

Did she seriously expect him to love her when his taste ran to svelte goddesses?

'Oh, come on, Sandrine.' An American accent this time. 'You can't know that. I say it was love at first sight. You just have to look at her to know she's head over heels in love with him. I think it's sweet.'

Imogen pressed a hand to her suddenly queasy stomach. She needed to keep moving. She didn't want to hear the speculation about her marriage.

Before she could move, Sandrine shrugged. 'I couldn't agree more. I feel sorry for the poor little thing.' Her voice dropped and the woman with her leaned closer.

Despite her resolve to move on, Imogen found herself waiting with bated breath.

'Didn't you see the photo in that scandal rag a month or so ago? Thierry kissing some blonde in a hotel bar when he was supposed to be on a climbing trip? The way he held her, it was obvious they'd just got out of bed.'

'Imogen. There you are. I was hoping to find you.' Startled, Imogen swung round to see Poppy Chatsfield beside her. The tall, red-headed model was another of the sophisticated set but her smile was warm.

Imogen blinked, trying to focus. Her stomach heaved and she almost stumbled as the floor rippled beneath her. A chill clamped her spine, freezing each vertebra in turn.

Thierry kissing another woman.

Thierry holding another woman...

'Imogen?' A hand gripped her elbow and she found herself ushered to the side of the room. 'You need to sit. In your condition you shouldn't be standing so long.'

A ragged laugh escaped Imogen's lips as Poppy led her to an antique sofa. 'Does *everyone* here know I'm pregnant?'

'Of course not.' Poppy sat beside her. 'But Thierry and

Orsino are old friends; he just told us the news. I came to congratulate you.' She paused, her concerned gaze roving Imogen's face. 'Can I get you something? Water? I found sipping it slowly sometimes helped the morning sickness.'

'No. I'm okay.' Imogen felt her mouth stretch in a grimace. Okay? How could she be okay? If what Sandrine had said was true… She wrapped her arms around her midriff, holding in the searing hurt.

'If you'll take my advice, you won't pay any attention to Sandrine.'

Imogen's gaze met Poppy's and heat washed her face. How many people had heard?

Poppy went on, her voice soft. 'I don't know what she said but I have a good idea it's what made you feel sick.'

Despite the haze of hurt and disappointment, Imogen found herself liking this woman.

'That's better. You look less like you're going to faint.'

'That's not going to happen.' Imogen straightened, drawing breath and putting a hand to her hair. 'But thank you. I appreciate your concern.'

Poppy nodded. 'You should know, Sandrine is—'

'I know. Years ago she and Thierry were an item.'

'Actually, I was going to say Sandrine isn't a complete witch, even if she's not at her best tonight. She's piqued because you married Thierry.'

'Why should she be piqued? She rejected him. She's been married to someone else for years.'

'Yes, and in all that time she's had the satisfaction of seeing Thierry go from one woman to another, never settling. As if he couldn't get over her.' Poppy nodded. 'Imagine how she feels after years thinking his heart was hers. Now you come along, stealing him. It's obvious he's fallen for you.'

Imogen pressed her hands together, wishing she could take comfort in Poppy's words.

Thierry hadn't fallen for her. He'd told her they were

well-matched because neither expected hearts and flowers and declarations of love.

Did that explain the other woman? Imogen swallowed convulsively at the thought of them together.

That must have been the weekend after they'd learned there'd been no need for them to marry because she was going to live. Imogen had known Thierry was rocked by the news, as she was, but he'd denied it.

A blonde. Sandrine had said brunettes weren't his type. Imogen's stomach churned so hard she thought she'd be ill. His taste ran to blondes like Sandrine and the woman in that bar.

Imogen stared blankly at the chattering crowd. How many had seen that photo? How many knew he'd betrayed her with another woman?

Clearly, Thierry didn't think it a betrayal—because he didn't love her, or because such things were accepted here? Did he expect her to put up with his affairs? Was that how he saw their marriage working?

This time the pain was a piercing white-hot blade to the heart.

'Imogen? You're worrying me. Shall I find Thierry?'

She jerked her head around to meet Poppy's stare. 'No,' she croaked. She couldn't face that yet. She needed time to digest this.

'I'm just…' Dazed, she searched for words to reassure Poppy. 'It's so crowded and close. I just can't get my breath.' It was true as far as it went.

Poppy squeezed her hand. 'You poor thing. I was the same when I was pregnant with Sofia.'

'If you'll excuse me, I'll head outside for some fresh air.' Imogen stood, locking her knees when they wobbled. She wasn't going to collapse in a pathetic heap, especially amongst Thierry's friends.

'I'll come with you.' Imogen was about to protest when Poppy whispered in her ear. 'You won't get far alone. Everyone wants to talk with you. If you're with me, you've got an excuse not to stop and chat.'

Minutes later Imogen rested her palms on the stone balustrade of the terrace. The buzz of the crowd was a muted hum and the high-riding moon washed the scene silver.

Imogen made herself turn to Poppy. 'That's better. Thank you. I'm okay now, so you can go back to Orsino. He's probably wondering where you are.' She was desperate to be alone.

Poppy waved a careless hand. 'No, he won't. He and Thierry are busy planning their grand trip.'

'Grand trip?' Imogen hadn't heard anything about a trip. But then she was probably the only person here who hadn't known about his other woman. Her fingers clenched on stone as revulsion welled.

'Oh, just the usual. For years they've been planning their next big adventure—the one they'll take as soon as Thierry's free.'

'Free?' The word tore from Imogen's choked throat. Free of her? She frowned. But then why insist they stay married?

'Free of the business.' Poppy bent her head, tsking as she disentangled her bracelet from a sequin on her dress.

'What do you mean, free of the business?'

Poppy looked up, astonishment on her features. 'You don't know?' She paused. 'Maybe I got it wrong,' she said quickly. 'I—'

'Please, Poppy. I need to know.'

Did Poppy hear the strain in her voice? Finally, she shrugged but she didn't look comfortable. 'Only close friends know. Thierry wouldn't talk about it in public.'

Clearly whatever *it* was, he hadn't thought to share it with his wife.

Disappointment hammered at Imogen's heart. She'd been fooling herself that if she was patient one day things would change between them!

How many secrets did Thierry hide?

'Thierry was dragged kicking and screaming into the family business when his grandfather became ill.'

Imogen nodded. 'He had a stroke.' She knew that, at least.

'Thierry hates being cooped up behind four walls—says it will send him crazy one day, being tied down. He vowed to set the company on its feet then step aside, find some good managers and take up his old life. He and Orsino used to do a lot of balloon treks together, rally driving too, and climbing.'

She paused, her glance darting to Imogen as if for confirmation she already knew this. Imogen said nothing, just turned to look at the cold, moonlit garden.

'For ages they've talked about a big trek to celebrate his freedom when it comes. Last I heard, it would be white-water rafting somewhere inhospitable. Somewhere you wouldn't catch me, ever. I'll stay where there are some creature comforts, thank you very much.'

Imogen recalled seeing Thierry across the crowd with Orsino Chatsfield. The two handsome, dark-haired men were easy to spot, given their height. But it was the animation on Thierry's face and the intensity of their conversation that she'd noticed.

Poppy turned towards her. 'Perhaps we could spend some time together when they're away? Get to know each other better?'

'That's a lovely idea.' Imogen forced the words out before her throat closed on a ball of wretched emotion. She liked Poppy. In other circumstances she could imagine them as friends. But it wasn't going to happen.

The pain morphed from a piercing stab to a heavy, slow-grinding ache pressing down, robbing her of air.

What more did she need to convince her this marriage was all wrong? He wasn't interested in settling down any more than he believed in love. He begrudged the time he spent in one place saving the family firm. How much more would he come to resent the woman and child who tied him down even further?

He'd put a good face on a bad situation. No doubt about it, her husband didn't shirk from what he believed to be his duty. Having met his grandparents, she realised he'd had responsibility drummed into him from an early age.

Something in her chest tore in an excruciating, slow-motion rip of anguish. Her heart?

'I'm afraid things are a little up in the air at the moment. A little...complicated.' She tried for a casual smile but knew it didn't convince, by the sombre way Poppy surveyed her.

'Of course. I don't mean to pressure you. A new marriage can be challenging as well as exciting.' Her laugh held a jarring note. 'Orsino and I went through hell before we worked out we loved and trusted each other.' She touched Imogen briefly on the arm. 'Just remember, if ever you need to talk, I'm available. I know how hard it can be, married to one of these take-charge men.'

'Thanks, Poppy. That's kind of you.' Imogen gulped, overcome by her empathy and kindness. She struggled for a lighter tone. 'I suppose we'd better get back inside before we're missed.' She couldn't think of anything worse. But she had her pride. She'd see the evening out then decide what to do.

Except she knew she'd run out of options.

She'd given her heart and soul to a man who didn't love her. Who could never love her. Who couldn't even give her his loyalty. He liked her, and he shared himself as much as he could with her, but ultimately she and their child were encumbrances, like the business he'd stepped in to save and couldn't wait to be rid of.

Her fond dream of him returning her feelings was just that—a dream.

There was only one thing any self-respecting woman could do. It was just a pity she hadn't done it months ago.

CHAPTER THIRTEEN

'IMOGEN?' THIERRY FLICKED on the light switch only to find his bedroom empty.

Where was she? She'd come upstairs when the last of the guests had left. There'd been fine lines of tiredness on her face yet that stubborn streak had seen her determined to play hostess to the end, despite his suggestion she retire early.

Thierry smiled. She'd been magnificent. He'd wondered if such a big function would be too much but she'd sailed through it with ease. Every time he'd looked over she'd been the centre of some eager group.

Afterwards he'd remained chatting with Orsino, who was staying with Poppy in one of the guest suites. It had been too long since they'd caught up. It was only now as work turned from manic to manageable that he realised how little he'd seen of his friends, as opposed to business contacts.

He marched across the room and opened the bathroom door. Empty. Where was she? His belly tightened in a premonition of trouble.

A few strides took him to the dressing room, but it too was empty. He scowled, thinking of her pale features as she'd headed upstairs and cursed himself for not seeing her to their room, despite her protests.

Thierry whipped around and back into the bedroom. Flicking off the light, he stepped towards the sitting room. That was when he noticed the strip of light under the adjoining bedroom door.

His heart slammed his ribs as he stopped mid-stride. What was she doing in her old bedroom? Incoherent thoughts jostled his brain. Was she ill? Was it the baby?

He wrenched open the door. The room looked peaceful in the glow of a bedside lamp and he heard water running in the bathroom.

He was almost at the bathroom door when he noticed the laptop open on the bed. One glance sent a sucker punch to the gut.

Thierry staggered, stared, and felt the world tilt.

Diable! Imogen had seen this? He went hot then cold as wave after wave of prickling remorse hit him.

He didn't want to, but Thierry took a step closer, then another. The photo was even worse close up. The blonde leaned into him, every line of her body taut and hungry as they kissed. From this angle, and with his hands at her waist, it looked like he'd been utterly lost to passion.

What had Imogen thought when she'd seen it? Flicking down the screen, scanning the snide little magazine commentary, he saw it was dated too. She'd have been in no doubt when this was taken.

His belly turned to lead. It was no good telling himself there'd been nothing in it. That didn't stop the guilt.

The door opened behind him, and his head flicked around.

'Hello, Thierry.' Imogen looked composed but pale.

'Are you all right?' He started towards her but stopped at the look on her face. Closed. Shuttered. Distant. He'd never seen her like that and it made something catch hard under his ribs.

'Why wouldn't I be?' She took off her watch and put it on the dressing table.

Thierry frowned. 'I was worried when you weren't in our room. What are you doing here?'

She shrugged as she moved things on the dressing table. Avoiding him? He stepped closer.

'I'm very tired and a bit queasy. I thought it better to sleep here.'

If she was tired, why wasn't she in bed?

The answer was easy: she'd been checking on him, trawling the media to find that incriminating photo. He tried to whip up indignation but found only regret.

'About that photo...' Her head swung round, her gaze meshing with his, and for a split second pure energy blasted through him, like he'd tapped into an electric current. 'It wasn't the way it looks.'

She walked past him and turned off the laptop, taking it to the dressing table.

'Imogen? I said it wasn't like it seems.'

'If you say so.'

'I do say so.' His fingers closed around her bare arm. The swish of her silky nightdress against his knuckles reminded him of the hours of pleasure they'd shared in his bed. It made her curious composure all the more disturbing. 'Why don't you say anything?'

Her eyes met his, more brown than green now and strangely flat.

'I'm tired. Can't we talk in the morning?'

'You've got to be kidding.' She'd seen that photo and withdrawn as if he were a stranger. Anger stirred. It was more palatable than the guilt lining his belly. 'We need to talk now.'

Her mouth flattened. 'I've had enough for one night.'

But instinct told him he couldn't delay. Keeping his hold on her arm, he led her to the bed. Her chin jutted mutinously but she said nothing as he sat beside her.

'Aren't you curious about the woman in the photo?' If he'd seen a picture of her in the arms of another man he'd have been more than curious. He'd want to rip the guy's arms off.

'Not particularly.' Her blank tone didn't match the fire in her eyes.

'She kissed me.' Thierry felt a shudder pass through her. 'I was drinking in the bar the last night of the climbing trip—'

'You don't have to justify yourself.'

But he did. He couldn't bear for her to believe he'd been with someone else. 'She asked for a drink then she kissed me.'

'I'm sure it happens to you all the time.' The hint of a snarl in her tone stirred tentative hope. Anger he could deal with. It was this…*nothing* that scared him.

'Nothing happened, Imogen. Just a kiss. What you saw was me pushing her away.'

Hazel eyes held with his, searching, then Imogen looked away. He felt her sag. 'If you say so.'

'I *do* say so.' How could he convince her? Her listlessness scared him. Where was his vibrant Imogen? Why wasn't she reacting? Even to hear her yell would be a relief.

'Right. Now that's cleared up, I'm going to sleep.'

Thierry stared. 'What's going on, *chérie*?'

'Don't!' She stiffened. 'Don't call me that.' She yanked her arm free and shuffled along the bed, putting distance between them. Her hand came up to cradle the spot where he'd held her, as if he'd hurt her, though his touch had been careful.

'I'm not your *chérie* and I never will be.'

'What are you talking about?' His pulse hammered a tattoo of fear. 'Of course you are. You're my wife.' He didn't like where this was going. He'd never seen her act so.

'A convenient wife—not your dear or your sweetheart, or whatever the translation is.' She waved her hand dismissively, and Thierry felt a plummeting sensation in his belly. 'I know it's just a word, a little nothing that slips out easily, but…' She turned her profile to him. 'But I don't want your casual endearments.'

'Imogen—'

'And since you insist on talking now…' she turned to him '…you should know I've decided to leave. This isn't working.'

Thierry shot to his feet, stalking across the thick carpet.

'Because of one stupid photo? I explained that. Nothing happened! I give you my word.' He squared his shoulders. A Girard's word was rock-solid, unquestionable.

She didn't look impressed. She hugged her arms around her, and he had to work not to let his gaze linger on her breasts, straining against her nightgown. 'It's not because of the photo.'

He strode across to loom over her so she had to arch her neck to look at him. 'Don't lie, Imogen.' Pain settled like a weighted blanket. 'We've always had the truth between us.' It was one of the things he'd most appreciated about her. She was direct and open, someone he could believe in.

'You want the truth?' Abruptly, the blankness was gone and heat shimmered in her eyes. 'The truth is marrying you was the biggest mistake of my life. I've had enough and I'm going home. I've booked a flight to Australia. Once I'm there I'll see about a divorce.'

The light dimmed and for a second Thierry's vision blurred, like the time he'd almost knocked himself out on a ski run in Austria. He braced himself, bending his knees slightly to counteract the sensation that he was swaying.

Yet nothing counteracted the horrible clogging in his chest, or the fierce pain slicing through his gullet.

'You're not going anywhere.' He didn't consciously form the words. They simply shot from his stiff lips.

'You're going to stop me by force?' Her eyebrows rose, giving her a haughty look that reminded him of his grandmother at her most disapproving. But his grandmother had never struck fear into him as Imogen did.

He stumbled back then steadied himself. 'I won't let you go.'

In a slither of fabric, she rose, standing toe to toe with him. 'You can't stop me.'

He shook his head, trying to fathom what had happened. Only hours ago everything had been fine.

'You know I can.' His voice was low and urgent and

when he touched her cheek he felt as well as heard her sudden intake of breath. 'We're good together, Imogen. You can't seriously want to give that up.'

Her head reared back and his hand fell. 'Sex?' She sneered. 'Yes, that's good. But why would I uproot myself just for that? It was a mad idea to think of staying in France.'

Thierry's eyes widened at her determination, and fear engulfed him. More than that. Fear was what he'd felt in the accident that had ended his Olympic skiing career. And the time his parachute had jammed before finally releasing.

This was more. This was on a level he'd never experienced. It was slow, grinding terror. Instead of creating a surge of defiant adrenalin that gave him courage to face danger, this weakened his very bones.

It made him feel…helpless.

'You think this is just about *sex*?' He saw her flinch and realised his voice had risen to a roar.

Thierry backed up, astonished at his loss of control. He never shouted. He never lost control. But he'd never felt anything like this visceral dread.

Before he could apologise she spoke, so softly and steadily the contrast with his own exclamation shamed him. 'If this relationship isn't about sex, tell me what it *is* about, Thierry.'

Her gaze held his gravely, and he swallowed. He flexed his hands.

'Our child…'

She dropped her eyes, her shoulders sagging before that bright hazel gaze met his again. 'Our child will do very well without this. It doesn't need us to live together in a farce of a marriage to be happy and healthy. I'd never try to cut you out of its life.'

So, he was to be a long-distance parent? Outrage flared.

'A farce? There's nothing farcical about this marriage, Imogen.' Fury leavened the horror. After all he'd done, all he offered, that was what she thought of them together? 'It's real. As real as French law can make it.' As real as *he* could make it.

'I don't care about the law, Thierry.' She folded her arms. 'I care about the fact I've married a man who doesn't love me. Who can never love me.' Her eyebrows rose as if in challenge. 'I want more. It was a mistake thinking I could settle for less.'

'I told you I didn't sleep with that woman.' This time, instead of anger, he felt desperation. Why wouldn't she believe him?

She shook her head. 'This isn't about her. This is about the fact you'll never really want *me*. Not for myself, just for the heir I'm providing, and because physically we're compatible.'

Imogen paced to the window, and Thierry tracked her with his eyes, willing down the need to haul her close and seduce her into forgetting this nonsense. Seduction wouldn't work this time.

His gut clenched in panic.

'We talked about this.' He kept his voice low and persuasive. 'We've got the basis of a great marriage.'

'No!' This time the shake of her head splayed dark tresses around her shoulders. 'I've changed, Thierry. Once upon a time I'd have been willing to put up with second best, with not quite achieving the dream. Once I didn't dare to dream because I was too busy being cautious. But thinking I was dying gave me courage.' She paused, a wistful smile curving her lips.

'So did you, Thierry. You helped me to be brave. You encouraged me to follow my dreams.' She hefted a breath that lifted her lovely breasts. 'My dream is to love and be loved. As simple and as huge as that.'

She rubbed her hands up her arms as if cold. Did she too feel the draught of icy air coursing around him?

'I understand you'll never love me, Thierry. You explained you don't believe in romance. Plus, I'm not the woman for you. I'm not blonde or sophisticated.' She shrugged. 'The woman you met in Paris wore borrowed plumage, just like tonight, and pretended to fit in, though she knew she was an outsider. I don't belong in your world, so it's better I go.'

'To find a man to love?' The words grated from his throat, leaving it raw.

Her face twisted with what looked like anguish. Except *he* was the one being torn apart.

'If I can.'

He stalked forward, grabbing her hands. They were cold. He looked down at her small, capable fingers in his and knew he couldn't bear to release her. It was asking too much.

'No.' His voice was a scrape of sound.

'Sorry?'

'You can't do that.'

Thierry watched his thumbs trace a possessive path across her knuckles. He imagined their hands together in twenty years, forty years, veined and wrinkled. The image made him feel…right inside. The idea of Imogen giving herself to another man, growing old with *him* instead, turned Thierry's stomach.

'You can't do it to me.'

'To *you*?'

Thierry met her questioning eyes. Instantly heat, recognition and emotion slammed into him. All those feelings that had been growing since the night he'd looked across a crowd in Paris and seen Imogen.

At first he'd thought it simple attraction, sexual desire with a dollop of curiosity and vicarious pleasure in watching her wide-eyed excitement at so many new experiences. But his feelings went way beyond that. They had almost from the first.

She tugged to free herself and his grip tightened.

'Let me go, Thierry.' Desperation laced her words. It gave him hope when moments ago there'd been none. There must be a reason she sounded as desperate as he felt.

'I can't.' It was the simple truth. How had she put it? *Simple and huge.* The truth was so huge it felt like he'd swallowed the sun.

Thierry met his wife's eyes, willing her to believe, to understand, to share what he felt. 'I can't, Imogen, because I love you.'

Thierry's hands on hers kept her standing as the room whirled. His arm came around her, strong and sure. Yet it was the look in his eyes that held her immobile. A look she'd never seen.

How was that for wishful thinking?

'Don't lie, Thierry.' She choked on the words.

He held her gaze, and she could almost believe she read desperation there. Enough to feign love now he realised it was what she wanted?

'I don't lie, Imogen.' He spoke gravely.

How badly she wanted this to be true! Enough to half-believe him, though it defied logic. 'I can't take any more, Thierry. Not tonight.'

'This can't wait.' Before she knew it she was high in his arms, cradled against his chest. She tried to be strong, but found her cheek nestling against him. His unique scent filled her. If this was the last time he held her she was determined to commit every detail to memory.

He moved, and her heart hammered, but he wasn't carrying her to bed. She was grateful. He'd be hard to resist if he tried to seduce her. Surely it was relief, not disappointment, she felt when he settled on the window seat, cradling her?

'I love you, Imogen.' The words vibrated through his body into hers. They wafted warm air in her hair.

'Thierry. Please.' She swallowed pain. 'Don't pretend. I won't stop you seeing our baby. You'll still have access.'

'This isn't about the baby. It's about us.'

Imogen turned her face into his chest, absurdly seeking comfort from the very man she shouldn't. 'It's not about us. This is pride speaking. You just don't want to let go.' Not after he'd shown his bride to his friends and all those society people.

'Of course I won't let you go. Not without a fight. It's taken a lifetime to find you.'

Shock caught her throat. Sincerity throbbed in every word. But it couldn't be.

Tilting her head, she leaned back enough to see him. Tension accentuated the planes and angles of that remarkable face. His mouth was grim, but his eyes looked lost. Surely not!

'Don't play games, Thierry.' Her voice scraped. 'It's cruel. That's not you.'

His arms tightened. 'What would be cruel is losing you. I love you, Imogen. Nothing matters but that.'

Her heart thudded in her throat and there was a rushing in her ears. 'You don't believe in love. You told me.'

'I was an arrogant, ignorant fool.' He brushed her cheek with a touch so tender it made her eyes well. 'Don't cry, Imogen. I want you to be happy.'

She opened her mouth to tell him she'd be happy if he released her. But it wasn't true.

'I'm not your type. I'm not tall and glamorous or—'

'You're so much my type I don't think I could live without you.' Her heart squeezed. 'As for me chasing blondes…' He shook his head. 'My tastes have matured. I never loved any of them.'

'Not even Sandrine?'

His mouth twisted. 'Does it make me sound old if I admit that was youthful folly? I was besotted but I'm glad she married someone else. We'd have made each other unhappy. We're too alike, too self-centred.'

'You're not.' His care for her had been anything but.

'I am. Now I've found you, I'll do anything to keep you.'

'Like pretend to love me.'

He cupped her cheek, holding her so she couldn't look away.

'There's no pretence. From the first you were different. I didn't know how or why but I felt it. Didn't you?' He barely paused. 'I told myself you were a breath of fresh air, a diversion, but you were much more. I was on the point of trying to find your address in Australia when you appeared at my office.'

'Really?' Her breath stilled.

'Really. I didn't know I was in love. Obviously I'm a slow learner. But it's true. I've been falling for you since that night in Paris.'

Hope vied with disbelief, stealing her words, jumbling her thoughts.

'But the woman you met in Paris wasn't the real me. I'm boring and—'

A crack of laughter stopped her. 'Boring? Anything but. You're more exciting than anyone I know.'

Imogen shook her head. 'You don't understand.'

'I understand. You're cautious, you like to weigh your options. You love numbers and order. But there's more. That woman in Paris is just another side to your personality, even though you suppressed her for years. You weren't pretending, just letting her loose.' His smile was so tender her heart turned over. 'Your zest for life is contagious and you help me be the man I want to be. The thought of losing you…' To her amazement, his voice cracked.

'Thierry?'

'Don't ever say you're not glamorous.' The authoritative confidence was back in his voice. 'You're the most gorgeous woman on the planet, whether you're in a ballgown, or old jeans or nothing.' His voice dipped. 'Preferably nothing.'

'Now you're lying,' she gasped.

He smiled. 'You're the most extraordinary woman in the world. I love you, Imogen. Stay with me and in time maybe you'll love me back.'

Her heartbeat snagged. He truly didn't know?

'But you don't want a wife to tie you down. You want freedom. A life of adventures like the one you're planning with Orsino.'

He shook his head. 'Before you I pined for what I'd lost—the freedom to take off at a moment's notice. I told myself I hated the job I'd been forced to do and it was true in the beginning. But I've come to realise I enjoy commerce. I like the cut and thrust of it, sizing up opportunities and making the most of them.' His smile was self-deprecating.

'I've had to do a lot of growing up recently. From self-absorbed playboy to responsible adult. It was hard but I'm happy with the outcome.' Thierry's thumb stroked her cheek. 'I'd already decided I need balance in my life. Now the business is on track, I can step back a little and have a life outside the office. But I don't want to step back totally. I want to run the business and find time for a little climbing or ballooning. But what I want most of all…' His voice dipped to that low, earthy note that always thrilled her. 'Is to be with you and our baby.'

Thierry paused, his gaze meshing with hers. Imogen felt hope and excitement pound through her. 'That's going to be the most exciting adventure of my life. I wouldn't miss it for anything.' His thumb brushed her cheek.

'I'll give it all up, the treks, the business, whatever, if it means you'll stay with me. I'll move to Aus—'

Imogen put her hand to his lips. They were warm and soft, at odds with his harsh expression. 'You'd do that? Give up all this?'

'I love you, Imogen.' His lips moved against her hand, his words balm to her aching heart. 'All I want is to be with you. The rest is nothing.'

The *château*, the place in society, the birthright, were less precious than her?

'Ah, *mon coeur*, don't cry. Please, it breaks my heart.'

He leaned in to kiss the hot tears sliding down her cheeks, and she bit back a sob. Her heart felt too full, as if it were going to burst.

She clutched his shoulders, trying to reassure herself this was real. 'You mean it?'

'I've never been more serious about anything in my life.' His expression was so solemn, so earnest. 'Stay with me and I'll prove it to you. No man could ever love you more than I do and one day, I hope, you'll feel the same way about me.'

Fire caught Imogen's throat as she smiled through her tears.

'Not *one day. Now.*'

He stared blankly as if he couldn't make sense of her words.

She slid her hands up to cup the back of his head, a quiver of excitement filling her at the knowledge dreams really did come true.

'I'm in love with you, Thierry. I have been since Paris. Since that first night.' She waited for his satisfied smile. Instead, she read shock then wonder on his proud features. 'You swept me off my feet, my darling.'

He closed his eyes, murmuring something in French under his breath that sounded heartfelt and urgent. When he opened them again she caught the dark gleam of excitement she'd loved from the beginning.

'You truly love me?'

She nodded. 'That's why I was so miserable, so ready to leave. I thought I could love you and live with you even though you didn't return my feelings. But then—'

'Then you thought I was a selfish, ungrateful brute who didn't understand what a treasure I had in you.'

Suddenly he swooped her up in the air then deposited her on the window seat. Before she could catch her breath he knelt before her, drawing her hands into his.

'Thierry? What are you doing?'

Midnight eyes held hers, and she couldn't look away, for they were filled with love. The same love welling inside her.

'Imogen, will you make me the happiest man in the world? Will you marry me and live with me for the rest of our lives?'

'But we're already married.'

'I want to marry you again—properly this time. With us both giving our hearts. A marriage of love, not convenience.'

'Oh, Thierry!' She blinked back fresh tears.

'You don't like the idea?' He frowned.

'I love the idea! I can't think of anything I'd like more.'

His loving smile, his tender kiss on her palm, told her he felt the same, but there was a mischievous glint in his eyes. 'Women love shopping for wedding dresses and the trimmings for a big wedding.'

'A big wedding?' She pretended to pout. 'What if I want to get married in a hot-air balloon or—'

His kiss stopped her words. When he pulled back he was grinning. 'Whatever you want, *mon coeur.* Perhaps we could go somewhere more comfortable to discuss the options.'

Imogen felt that smile to the soles of her feet. 'You have the best ideas, Thierry.' She put her hand in his and let him draw her to her feet, knowing he was right. The future together would be the adventure of their lifetimes.

* * * * *

Also available in the
ONE NIGHT WITH CONSEQUENCES
series this month
BOUND TO THE TUSCAN BILLIONAIRE
by Susan Stephens

And look out for THE SHOCK CASSANO BABY
by Andie Brock in May 2016.

#3421 A DIAMOND DEAL WITH THE GREEK

by Maya Blake

Arabella "Rebel" Daniels would rather skydive naked than agree to Draco Angelis's outrageous suggestion. But, unbeknownst to Rebel, her father embezzled money from the formidable magnate, and now *she* must pay back the debt by whatever method Draco demands!

#3422 INHERITED BY FERRANTI

by Kate Hewitt

It's been seven years since Sierra Rocci left Marco Ferranti on the eve of their convenient wedding. But now that she's back in Sicily, Marco needs Sierra's help with his latest business venture and is determined to claim their wedding night!

#3423 ONE NIGHT TO WEDDING VOWS

by Kim Lawrence

Lara Gray is consumed by the passion awakened within her after one night with Raoul Di Vittorio. But what she doesn't know is that Raoul needs a temporary wife, and he thinks Lara is the ideal woman for the job!

#3424 THE SECRET TO MARRYING MARCHESI

Secret Heirs of Billionaires

by Amanda Cinelli

Read all about Italian billionaire Rigo Marchesi's secret love child with London actress Nicole Duvalle. This bombshell could destroy CEO Rigo's latest business deal. Unless the rumors that the baby scandal will have a fairy-tale ending are true?
